Departing Vienna

To Nick & Dave
With best wishes
John Taylor

Departing Vienna

J.M. Taylor

forbitou

Published by Forbitou Books

43 Caldervale Road
London
SW4 9LY

© J.M. Taylor 2014

The moral right of J.M. Taylor to be identified as the author of this work has been asserted by him in accordance with the Copyright, Designs and Patents Act of 1988.

A CIP Record for this book is available from
The British Cataloguing-in-Publication Data Office

ISBN 978-0-9554860-1-2

All rights reserved. No part of this publication may be reproduced, stored in a retrieval system, or transmitted at any time or by any means electronic, mechanical, photocopying, recording or otherwise, without the prior written permission of the copyright owner and of the publisher.

This novel is entirely a work of fiction. The names, characters and incidents portrayed in it are the work of the author's imagination. Any resemblance to actual persons, living or dead, events or localities is entirely coincidental.

Text design and typesetting by Etica Press

Cover design by Leyland Gomez

Printed and bound by CPI Group (UK) Ltd, Croydon, CR0 4YY

For CBT

who first heard the story

Part I

Translations are like wives –
Either plain and faithful or beautiful and treacherous.

Edmund Jaloux

One

Resch left Gestapo Headquarters in Morzin Platz and headed towards the Donau Kanal. A physical and mental numbness reduced him to an automaton. He paused on the Marien Brucke and stared down at the glutinous waters of the canal. Slowly his fear began to ebb away, to be replaced by a horror of the future. A thin mist flowed slowly with the sluggish water. With an effort, Resch continued across the bridge and up Lilienbrunn Gasse. His leaden footsteps echoed in the street which even at this early evening hour was almost deserted. Gradually his mind cleared as the light faded in the gloaming ... dusk ... sunset ...or perhaps even fading crepuscular light?

Mark Shilton got up from his desk, glanced at the cold dregs of coffee in his cup and stood looking out of the tall window. The leaves of the plane trees were now fully open and casting their shade on the scabs and scales of the trunks. A train hooted in the distance and then the sound of carriages clattering over points filtered softly into his consciousness. Although the line was far off, at certain times of the day these noises penetrated between the narrow North London streets, reflected off end of terrace walls and transmitted by some chance of acoustics.

Translating prose was so different from translating poetry, he mused. He had found recasting a poem into a different language challenging but creative in a way that empowered him while attempting to respect the poet. This prose demanded more accuracy and adherence to the exact meaning of the original but equally the author's voice needed to be preserved but in another language. How to choose the English word which would both express the original intention and yet not set up different nuances for the English reader? The original had a strong Viennese flavour, in its lilt and occasional slang. A parody of Austrian vernacular would be absurd but to flatten the sense and sound of these singing sentences would do a deep disservice to the author.

At moments like this, Mark almost regretted accepting the assignment. It was in that late Spring of 1988 that Gillian Marshall at the publishers had asked him to come in to discuss a project and he had made his way across Byng Place towards Gordon Square. The Bloomsbury offices of the Thalia Press had occupied a scruffy Georgian townhouse since its inception in the '60s by Aubrey Newberg, publishing new literary fiction, and in its early days had nurtured some significant talents. Mark climbed the bare wooden staircase to Gillian's office and peered round the door. She looked up from her desk to note his scuffed suede shoes and tired jacket with its bulging pockets. They exchanged the look which only old lovers can, furtive yet distant, sharing a rueful nostalgia. The affair had been brief but intense and Mark had doubted whether Elizabeth had learned about it. Wives though can, through almost imperceptible variations in body language and inflexions, sense a betrayal. Afterwards the faint fissure running through their marriage remained invisible until the terrible seismic shock forced it open. A resurgent feeling of regret brought him back to the matter in hand.

"Come on in, Mark." With a laugh which acknowledged their old intimacy, she cleared a pile of books from a chair next to her desk. "I want to try this idea on you. You've done some great translating for us recently – those Trakl and Heym poems in the Central European anthology."

Mark was listening and trying to recall her fascination for him; her dark looks, a particular way her lips articulated words and the nervous flick of her head to displace a strand of hair.

"You've met Aubrey, haven't you? Well, he came up with this idea of combing through the back-lists of German and Central European publishers to find an undiscovered gem."

"How come this masterpiece hadn't been discovered the first time it was published?"

"Well, sometimes the first printing just didn't take off. Maybe the time, the readership, or whatever was just wrong. It's been done before, you know. Obscure titles have been translated into English and been a great success. The authors became world famous, though sadly, usually posthumously."

"OK, so Aubrey has discovered this forgotten masterpiece. How did he find it?"

"Well, we've got a young assistant, Helmut, on exchange from Herder, the big Frankfurt publishers. Herder have a branch in Vienna, originally a firm called Wallisch Verlag which Herder had taken over in the Sixties. Aubrey sent Helmut off to trawl through their archive."

"And you're going to tell me what young Helmut found."

"Yes, it's called *'Das Uberleben im Finsternis'*, which apparently means Survival in the Dark, or something like that, by Otto Bühler. Aubrey thought we might publish it as 'Hidden in the Shadows.'"

Mark decided not to correct her German pronunciation but looked at the book which she pushed across the desk towards him. It was a paperback, not very thick, with that simple, uninspired cover design of lettering which was typical of German and Austrian publishing just after the War before the marketing departments brought in the graphic designers. He thought he might have heard of Bühler, though he could not remember any details about him.

"So why me? I know you have other translators on your books who are more experienced with literary texts."

A slow flush reddened her neck and she looked distracted for a moment, "Well ... your Vienna experience and your knowledge of the pre-War literary scene there."

He wondered whether she had decided to offer him this piece of work out of some vague sense of guilt for the abrupt way in which she had ended their affair, having taken up with a picture dealer some years her junior.

"How do you and Aubrey know if it is any good?"

Gillian had recovered her poise, "We've had Gail Bisset at UCL have a look at it and she was quite impressed."

Mark knew Professor Bisset as an ambitious young academic specialising in mid-twentieth century German literature. "So what's the book about?" countered Mark.

Gillian picked up a note from her desk, "It's about the hiding of Jews from the Nazi authorities in Vienna during the Second World War."

"Aha, a 'good German' book, or in this case a 'good Austrian' story. So you reckon it's going to sell well?"

"Well, Aubrey does. Will you take it on?"

Mark paused for a moment. It was airless in the office with only the rhythmic hum of a photocopier on a landing to measure the silence against the background noise of the Bloomsbury traffic. Although he had plenty of work at the time, there was a gap between major assignments. He sensed a need for some injection of novelty into his work which an opportunity to tackle literary translation might provide.

"Alright, but I'll have to shift some of my other work and lay in the midnight oil." He liked to get his bid in early in negotiations.

"Hmm, I seem to remember it was more a matter of the midnight whisky but OK, we need to talk about an advance and a submission date."

One wall of the living room, which also served as his study, was lined with books and a careful inspection of his library, including his doctoral thesis, revealed little about Otto Bühler beyond the fact that he was a minor member of the Vienna literati in the 1930's. Intrigued, Mark set off across Hyde Park to Kensington Gore to consult the Austrian Cultural Institute and the Goethe Library. These sources provided only basic information. Bühler was born in 1914 and lived in Vienna. He had some poems published in Karl Kraus's journal, *Die Fackel*, and one included in an anthology published by Wallisch Verlag. Wallish also published a collection of short stories by Buhler entitled *'Die sternklare Kopfsteine'* – *'Starlight on the Cobbles'*. He died in 1947 at the age of 33 and his novel, *'Das Uberleben im Finsternis'* was published posthumously in 1955. One source in the Austrian Cultural Institute showed Bühler in a group photograph of editors and contributors to *Die Fackel*. He stared out of the photograph, a serious and determined looking young man in his twenties.

Mark had decided to read the book twice before getting down to any translation work. On a Friday morning he set all other tasks to one side and spent the day reading fast but with concentration in order to get a feel for the shape of the book and for its sounds, its rhythms and cadences. He had hardly finished the final chapter when he had to clear the papers from the table and lay two places for supper. He was frying the chicken when he heard the front door bell and rushed downstairs to help Ruth drag her bicycle into the hallway. She climbed the stairs ahead of him, tossed her leather jacket aside and after they had kissed on each cheek fell into an armchair, running her hands through her cropped hair. She looked tired and thinner than usual as Mark handed her a glass of wine, relieved that they would be together for the whole evening, her presence dispelling the pall of loneliness which crept over the flat on many evenings.

They had met six months before in a gallery off Queen Square at a poetry reading. Mark, surveying the crowd, had seen her across the room, an intriguing lost profile. Suddenly she had turned and although Mark had tried to look away she held his stare for a moment. After the reading, when the poet had acknowledged the brief burst of applause, he went over to the book table and flipped through a copy of the poet's latest collection.

"Are you going to buy it?" He turned to find her standing next to him.

"I don't know." He leant towards her, "So often my enthusiasm ebbs away after the event – another unread tome staring accusingly from the bookcase."

She laughed and they drifted away looking idly at some of the lurid pictures in the gallery. He had glanced at her as she squinted at a canvas of vivid swirls with her head slightly to one side. "I'm hungry – join me for a meal round the corner? There's a passable Italian place I know."

She had chatted easily over their plates of pasta, finding a shared interest in contemporary theatre, but not Pinter, and an appetite for jazz and Bach. After the meal he had walked with her to the Tube station and before they parted they agreed to meet again. She gave him a quick kiss on the cheek and, after passing through the turnstile, looked back with a slightly ironic grin and raised her hand in farewell. He had strolled away and despite the chill November wind had found himself humming a half remembered tune while leaves were swept past him and upward. A pattern had emerged over the following weeks. Ruth would come to supper on Friday evenings when she was not visiting her parents in Hampstead and once a month or so they would spend Sunday together at an exhibition or walking over the Heath. Some ten years younger than Mark, he learnt little over the weeks about her past. She had been at London University and then taken up teaching. While still a student, she had an affair with a member of the Socialist Workers Party but that, as she insisted, was another story. He was drawn by her air of appealing fragility which belied her tough determination although it was only later that he discovered this was a further protective layer.

On Monday, Mark read *Das Uberleben im Finsternis'* again, slowly and carefully, noting characters and events, and considering the phrases and words which gave it its flavour. For an author with a literary background of poetry and short stories, the style was terse and direct with a strong sense of Vienna in the late Thirties and during the War. The feel was more thriller or crime novel than literary and had a pace and vividness which drew Mark through the plot. The first part of the novel established the two protagonists, Gustav Zeimer and Emile Resch, the former being the primary narrative voice. As the deportation of Jews from Vienna gets underway, the two friends decide to hide Jewish families. Resch is put under pressure by the Gestapo and betrays those he is hiding. He is stricken with remorse and commits suicide. Zeimer manages to evade discovery and gets his Jewish girlfriend to safety in Switzerland. Mark could see the attraction of the story of a 'good Austrian' and it fell into what was almost becoming a genre of saviours during the Holocaust; the Righteous as they became known.

He felt a surge of enthusiasm for the task ahead. This might be not just a technical assignment but a role for a translator to make known a story, albeit fictional, that had historical significance. Moreover if the resulting translation was well received, it would be another enhancement to his career and well established status as a Germanist, despite the traditional role of the translator as the grateful and ever obsequious servant of the publishing industry. He looked forward to working on fiction as a relief from his usual diet of academic texts, occasional biographies, and political memoires.

He leant back in his chair, listening to the small sounds of the flat; the creaks of the radiator pipes, the muffled radio in the flat below and stiletto heels on the pavement below. In the early years, the relief of living on his own had been palpable although the deeply repressed grief, granite hard around his heart could still erupt in a geyser of emotion triggered merely by a chord of music, chance phrase or the cry of a gull. But latterly the silence had become oppressive and he had resorted to taking up his saxophone, relic of student days, although respect for the neighbours forced him to play in the bathroom.

Five weeks later, Mark's initial enthusiasm had been blunted by the daily battle to be true to the original while creating an engaging version which reflected the character of the author's voice and a sense of historical place. The rhythms and inflections of Viennese Austrian were difficult to transpose into English without descending into caricature. The little ironies were unintelligible in another language and the racy romanticism of some passages could sound false and overblown. He was searching for an English style which would match that of the author; perhaps Le Carré or Grisham. He needed a different style from his own which had been developed to cope with technical, non-fiction texts.

Frustrated and a little depressed, given the scale of the task ahead, he decided to talk to Jeremy Garforth. Mark knew he could be found every Tuesday afternoon holding court in the Senior Common Room of the University's Senate House. As he walked across Gower Street, he hoped that Orwell's great white tower of the

Ministry of Truth would provide some guidance. Mark paused at the entrance to the room. Jeremy was seated at a circular table surrounded by a small group of postgraduate students, which inevitably included two good looking young men. Mark had known him for some thirty years; his dark tousled curls showed only a few strands of grey although his body had filled out since his days as a college rugger player. He was still dressed in his '60s attire; purple shirt and wine coloured corduroy jacket.

Jeremy had been Mark's supervisor for his doctoral thesis all that time ago. Only five years older than Mark, he had become his respected mentor; part hero, part father figure, with his expansive, extravert personality. He remembered how he had gently to rebuff Jeremy's tactile overtures so that eventually it was understood that their relationship would remain academic and platonic. Later, Jeremy had married an older colleague but it was only a short lived arrangement and over the years he had shared a flat in Fitzrovia and a louche lifestyle with a succession of younger men, one of whom had been Aubrey Newberg. He and a friend had bought a house in the Italian Marche and in the past had invited Mark to stay but he had always declined, fearing that he would feel uncomfortable in the milieu of Jeremy's circle. He had remained a loyal counsellor, helping Mark obtain commissions, providing references and introducing him to university presses and to Thalia. He had been a key influence in developing Mark's career and he owed him much but sometimes friendship can be diminished by such debts. Now, with his group of acolytes gathered around him, he was making some knowing remark while laying a plump hand on the tanned and muscled forearm of a handsome young man at his side.

"Ah, Mark, dear boy!" he grinned with delight as the group dispersed. Mark eased himself into a chair at the table and launched into an explanation of the project, while Jeremy interjected a few questions. "So, how is the actual business of translation going? And this gem from the Danube, why has it lain undiscovered for so long?"

Mark told the story of the discovery of the text in an old Viennese backlist and how the early part of the book told of Zeimer and Resch's early life, their involvement in the activities of the Socialist party and the growing threat from Nazism, especially after the Anschluss.

"But why did this Bühler chap write this book at that moment and then promptly die?"

"I don't know yet. He must have known about Jews being hidden in Vienna during the War but his actual motive seems obscure. It's a posthumous publication, so lots of unanswered questions. And he seems to have died suddenly of a heart attack or something similar, fairly young." Mark then ran through a list of technical problems he was wrestling with in translating the novel.

"Yes, I can see the difficulties," Jeremy drummed a pencil on the low table, "In a way it's easier with poetry. Maybe it's, in one sense, an impossible task. Even with prose, you're creating a new entity, a successor in a new language for a different culture. A translation tries to be true to its inheritance but in the end, like all children, it repudiates its parent! But don't worry. If the author is as good as Aubrey says he is, the vitality and rhythms will survive."

As they talked, Mark remembered him as a young lecturer who had guided and shaped his early research and writing. His initial plan for his thesis on Freud's influence on Schnitzler and Weiss had been bent and changed by Jeremy's powerful and persuasive arguments to a broader look at the Viennese literary scene during the inter-War years. Mark's youthful enthusiasm and sense of treading new and untrammelled pastures had been diluted and eventually dulled.

By getting up early, Mark was able to maintain steady progress while continuing proof reading a translation of a Berlin conference report. The pages of completed translation continued to mount but many were covered in deletions, amendments in coloured inks, or strips of paper stapled over passages which did not seem to express what Bühler was meaning, or what Mark believed he was trying to say. One Friday evening as they grappled with their noodles in a Japanese restaurant after an evening at Ronnie Scott's, he poured out all his concerns to Ruth, itemising all the obstacles and difficulties he had met with during the week. Despite an exhausting week at school, she listened sympathetically. She seemed fascinated by the plot, asking why the two main characters had decided to hide their Jewish acquaintances and how they had managed to evade the authorities.

She paused with her chopsticks in the air. "What was the pressure on Resch which made him betray the family he had been looking after?"

"Well, Resch has a girlfriend whose brother works for the Gestapo. She is recruited as an informer but warns Resch that he is under suspicion. The only way for him to avoid arrest and torture is to betray the Jewish family."

"What about the other character? Is he compromised as well?"

"Not really. Zeimer is alerted to Resch's betrayal and succeeds in moving his hidden Jews, including his girlfriend, to safety – he goes underground for a while."

"And Resch?"

"He is crushed with guilt and commits suicide. Meanwhile, Zeimer smuggles to get his girlfriend to safety in Switzerland."

"It's a pretty amazing story. I wonder where the author got his ideas from. I think some Jews were hidden in Vienna. Perhaps he was involved."

"If so, I am not quite sure why he wrote a novel about these events and not some factual account." Mark was helping Ruth into her jacket and apologised for ruining the evening with all his worries when it should have been a relaxing end to their working week.

Ruth thought for a moment and kissed him on the cheek. "You need to get closer to your author. Not easy as he is dead, but why not go to Vienna for, say, a week. Take a break – it would give you a chance for a bit of research there. But just to absorb the atmosphere too. You know – the feel of the place again. It's ages since you were there." She gave him a quick, warm hug. Mark agreed to think about the idea and she left with a cheery goodbye after unchaining her bicycle from a lamppost.

Mark had spent a year in Vienna at least thirty years before and his recollections of that time had receded into a catalogue of youthful memories, remote and disconnected from the present. Now a well respected translator, he was established by his early fifties, if not at the peak of his profession then at least as one who had built a solid reputation and was always in demand. Ruth's suggestion, which had at first seemed unrealistic, began, after some thought, to appear attractive. Even if no trace of Bühler was found, the trip would provide a change of air and even an opportunity to rediscover some of the places in the city which he barely remembered but which glowed with the soft affection of youth.

The Friday before Mark's trip to Vienna, Ruth stayed late as they chatted about a film at the Renoir which both had seen. A second bottle of wine was opened and eventually emptied. At first he had viewed their friendship as purely platonic, a balm to his lonely existence, but now he felt a growing need for a closer physical attachment. At his suggestion, Mark made up his bed with clean sheets for Ruth and curled up on the sofa in an old sleeping bag. Just the awareness of her sleeping there in his bedroom at the end of the short corridor allowed him to imagine a less desiccated future. He awoke late with a slight headache to the sounds of the radio and Ruth searching the cupboards for coffee. Suddenly the coming journey to Austria, together with their deepening relationship, melded with the sunlight filtering through the leaves of the plane trees to create a moment of expectation and hope which he had not felt for some years.

Two

Vienna in June was already hot and the Ringstrasse thronged with tourists. Mark hardly recognised the city, so different was it from his memories of 1957. Then he had arrived in late September, in an autumn which presaged the bitter cold of the winter months to come. Now the warm, sunlit streets and squares, the relaxed well dressed pedestrians and the carefully restored buildings were all at variance with his recollections of that grey capital thirty years ago, along whose deep canyon streets cold winds blew a fine dust, sending the inhabitants scurrying into their dark apartments. By nightfall the streets had been almost deserted but for some figure, a man in a hat, turning into a doorway. Scenes which had a de Chirico sense of mystery and foreboding, reminiscent of the Third Man. At the crossroads of Europe, the faded imperial capital of a small neutral country, which the Russians had left only a couple of years before, subsisted in the shadow of the Iron Curtain. Vienna could hardly believe in its own independence and freedom but remained reticent and cautious in case the tanks should move on across the Hungarian border. In his contacts with the University, he had become aware of a yawning absence in the intellectual and cultural life of the city, an absence which was never alluded to. All that the Jewish community had contributed to the arts and science was but a legacy tinged with an aura of silent guilt.

Now, thirty years later, Mark took a room in a cheap hotel near the Ring and started to re-orientate himself by bringing memory and reality together in a focus that altered both. He decided to search for the apartment in Hahngasse in the 9th District where he had lived all those years ago in a tiny room overlooking a light-well festooned in pigeon droppings. The entrance to the building seemed somehow different but inside the stairs were unchanged. He paused for a moment as he climbed to the third floor, suddenly remembering the intense loneliness of his year in the city. He had made no friends and few acquaintances, becoming increasingly isolated and thrown in on himself. He had even been driven to attend the English church but had drawn back from the patronising attention of the chaplain. Now, on arriving at the door of the apartment, he rang the bell which was answered by a woman wiping her hands on her apron. In response to his enquiries, she remembered the old couple who had looked after him in their silent, almost grudging way. The old man had died many years ago but his widow still lived in a nursing home in Heitzing, she believed.

He spent a day following routes of many years ago to the University and the library, and discovering that the cheap restaurants and bars he had frequented had become smarter and more expensive. He strolled beside the Ringstrasse, past opulent squares with views of elevated palaces, and suddenly recalled the Russian soldier on his column, known to the locals as the Monument to the Unknown Looter. Later, he paused for a beer at a table by the Donau Kanal and then found himself at the entrance to Morzin Platz. He suddenly recalled that Resch would have walked over the bridge from here after his interrogation, past the Diana baths, now replaced by the huge geometric shape of the IBM building.

He then resolved to begin his quest for any faint traces left by Bühler. Herder Verlag, the Frankfurt publishers, still had a branch in Vienna, a modern glass fronted building just off Parkring. It was here that Helmut had discovered *'Das Uberleben im Finsternis'* and it was just possible, Mark hoped, that someone might remember publishing the novel. The receptionist was doubtful but, after two telephone calls, arranged for an editor to come down and see Mark. After a short wait, a middle aged man appeared and introduced himself. Mark explained that he was hoping to meet someone who knew Bühler and his work. The editor apologised for not knowing of Bühler at all but after making further telephone calls from the reception desk, he returned with a slip of paper.

"No-one working here knows anything about this novel or its author. But an editorial assistant who worked here in the Wallisch days, and retired many years ago, perhaps might recall this author of former times. Her name in Frau Hanna Ornstein – here is her telephone number."

Mark thanked him profusely and went out into the street clutching the slip of paper as the first, and at that moment only, lead which might put him on the right track in his search. Back in his hotel he dialled the number. Hanna Ornstein, once she heard the details of Mark's request, sounded delighted and only too eager to talk about Bühler. She suggested that they meet at Cafe Prükl on Stubenring the next afternoon.

When Mark arrived at the cafe, it seemed that every table was occupied by two or three Viennese ladies of a certain age, wearing neat hats, and engaged in animated conversation. Standing at the entrance, he eventually noticed a table with a lone, older woman. She wore a dark green battered felt hat sporting a tattered feather and a grey herringbone suit with a cream blouse. Her clothes had the shabbiness of long use which suggested either constrained finances or a disregard for fashion. He made his way through the intricate arrangement of small marble topped tables, momentarily disoriented by the mirror clad walls which reflected multiple images of the waitresses in their black dresses and white aprons who whirled about the room in a complex dance. He reeled to her table.

"Frau Ornstein?"

"Yes? And you are Herr Shilton? Come, take a seat."

She turned to inspect him through thick round lenses. She smiled, touching his sleeve lightly and ordered coffee and two small slices of cake. Mark explained in more detail his task of translating Bühler's novel, his difficulties, and the reasons for his visit to Vienna. She listened to him in silence, looking up from her cake with a myopic and quizzical gaze.

"I am so happy that Otto Bühler is remembered after all these years. He had great talent but died so young. Now all his works are out of print and it is so wonderful that his late – his last and only – novel should be translated into English." Behind her thick glasses, her eyes sparkled. "You are indeed fortunate to find someone who remembered him. I became the unofficial Wallisch archivist after the take-over. They used to call me 'Buchmendel'."

"Ah, from that short story by Stefan Zweig! But this is not the same cafe."

"No – but I maybe Zweig's cafe was a mixture of many such places in the Twenties. So you know your Viennese literature. Now tell me more about yourself"

"Well, I'm not a 'man without qualities'."

Frau Ornstein gave a short explosive laugh. "And you have read your Musil – so we have the measure of each other. As you may guess, I was very fond of young Otto – in a motherly way for sure." She smiled and her eyebrows gave a twitch. "I can admit now that I was a little bit attracted to him – this serious, intense young man but with such a lively sense of humour." Her eyes closed momentarily and she drew a long breath at the memory of her young self. She shrugged and continued, "He was in essence a poet. He had some of his first, his very early, poems published in student magazines and in the Social Democratic Party literature. But his great breakthrough came when Karl Kraus published one of his pieces in *Die Fackel*. That's when I first came across him – and such talent." She shook her head in amazed memory as she manoeuvred a fork full of chocolate cake into her mouth. "I showed the poem to a director and told him that we should keep an eye on this young man. I arranged to meet him – and well! – he was so intense, so full of enthusiasm, he sparkled – no, crackled, you know, like electric sparks. Always talking fast with his mouth full of his favourite plum pastries. Anyway, we included three of his poems in an anthology of young poets – it must have been about '37.

"When did he start writing prose?"

"He was already writing short stories, very much in the style of Zweig. I really championed his cause and the next year or so – I don't remember exactly – we published this little volume of short stories by Otto – *'Die sternklare Kopfsteine'*. Not a big print run but it sold quite well." She paused for a moment and took a generous sip of coffee.

"And during the War?"

"Nothing – not a thing. I lost contact with him completely. And after the War I tried to make enquiries but there was no news of him." Mark played with the crumbs on his plate. Frau Ornstein's memories provided useful background to the early Bühler as a poet and short story writer but he was not yet any closer to the novel. Suddenly she looked up, "One day a colleague came into my office and showed me Otto's death notice in the Neue Freie Presse. I was so upset – I remember crying a little – there at my desk."

She sat in silence for a few moments but then gave a slight start, "'*Das Uberleben im Finsternis*' – what an extraordinary novel. But more extraordinary was its arrival."

"Its arrival – what do you mean?"

"It must have been about '47. A parcel arrived at work, addressed to me. Badly wrapped and tied up with crude string, you know, the sort of twine farmers use. Inside was the handwritten manuscript of Otto's novel. And with it was a simple note which said that Otto had passed away a few months previously but before he died had asked that the manuscript be sent to me."

"And who had written the note?"

"It was just signed 'a close friend'."

"Did you have any idea where it came from? Was it posted in Vienna?"

"It's strange that you should ask that." Frau Ornstein was silent for some moments and her eyes were moist behind her glasses. "I remember noting at the time that it had been posted near Salzburg. Yes, that was it – it was postmarked Bad Ischl – and I wondered 'why there?' He was always such a city boy."

"And what did you do with the manuscript?"

"What indeed – quite a history. I went to my director and told him that Bühler was dead but that we had a posthumous manuscript."

"And what happened – what did he think of it?"

"He looked at it, read it, and said 'a story about saving Jews in Vienna – this is not the place or the time to publish such a novel. It wouldn't sell and wouldn't be good for the House.' He was very protective of Wallisch. I should explain that the writers' organization was dominated by former Nazis and ultra-orthodox Catholics – they controlled all the state subsidies which we relied on."

"But I know it was published – by Wallisch – in 1955."

"Yes, indeed, and you are curious?" She turned a self-satisfied smile towards him. "I had been promoted to assistant editor due to the shortage of men after the War and I kept on and on at my boss, year after year, saying 'this is a good novel – maybe not great – but to honour the memory of Otto Bühler, and for the people of the new Austria, it should be published."

"So what finally persuaded him?"

"I suppose you could call it literary fashion – or just changing times. Germany was beginning to think about the War. Even to just think about it was a great step forward – Heinrich Böll was being published – by '55 many of his, so called, 'post-War' books had come out."

"The atmosphere had changed then?"

"I don't know about that. In those years, our emotions were still frozen – a sort of conspiracy to forget all that had happened. What we call *Vergangenheitswältigung* – working through the past – had barely begun and wouldn't really for another thirty years. Even today our President's War record is only just beginning to be questioned. There is still so much we have got to understand and accept about those times." She leaned forward and gripped his arm, gesturing with her eyes to the other tables where old ladies chatted eagerly over their lemon teas and cake. "These women know what their husbands did in the War – occasional slips of the tongue, odd references, murmuring in their sleep. When they died, their widows inherited half their pensions – and maybe more of their guilt."

With a shrug of her shoulders, she finished her coffee. "So finally *'Das Uberleben im Finsternis'* was published – I'm told it sold better in Germany than here," she sighed and gave Mark a smile of one who has been a little unburdened by a tale that needed to be told.

Mark thanked her profusely. "Who might be able to tell me more about Otto Bühler's life?"

Frau Ornstein thought for a moment. "Otto had a brother – Karl – who may still live here. I just might have his address – if I do, I will leave a message at your hotel."

Mark paid the bill and escorted her out onto the street where she lent heavily on her stick. "I give you my best wishes for your work of translation," and then, drawing herself up, "Be true to Otto Bühler; be true to his genius and to his memory. And could you please send me a copy of your translation when it is published. I do not read English well but it will be a memento – a sort of keepsake." She set off slowly but resolutely down the street.

After breakfast next morning, Mark looked over the notes he had made after his meeting with Frau Ornstein and enquired at the hotel reception desk if there was a message for him. As there was none, he set off to explore the maze of streets and alleyways that made up the Innenstadt. So much had changed, it was as if he had never walked the narrow ways before but occasionally an old building or view triggered a vague sense of return more than a distinct memory. The corner of St Stephen's Cathedral seen from a street corner or the stepped levels of Am Hof suddenly appeared familiar again. A stroll through the formal gardens towards the Hofburg palace finally led him back to the Ring and he found himself looking across at the great mass of the Kunsthistorische Museum.

On a whim, he climbed the steps of the grand entrance which led into the vast hall dominated by a great marble staircase. Mark had got to know the Museum well and it had become in some way a haven from the disappointments of his research in Vienna. Jeremy Garforth's diversion of his thesis away from his initial ideas had undermined his enthusiasm for the project. His research had proved more difficult that he had expected and his contacts at the University had been formal, suffering from the distant haughtiness of the Viennese academic bureaucracy. In that strange lonely year, the Museum had come to be a place where he could lose himself in its labyrinthine rooms and corridors. He often found himself in the picture galleries where the Emperors had created one of the finest collections in Europe. After he had been visiting the Museum for some months, he had discovered that there were weekly tours led by an art historian. The guide was a highly knowledgeable woman who could interpret and bring to life a painting in a way that transformed his understanding and appreciation. He recalled vividly the Breughel paintings of the seasons, of which the Museum held three of the series of seven.

On one tour, the guide assembled the group, mainly late middle aged women and a few tourists, before 'Winter' and had spoken with such passion and fluency for nearly half an hour that the painting reflected not only the season and times but even European history and philosophy. Now Mark was standing before the painting again and the guide's eloquent exposition came flooding back. He remembered her animation and the way her long auburn hair swept back and forth as she turned now to the group and then back to the painting. Despite searching his memory, her name evaded him. However, one element of the painting began to draw the past towards him. In the group to the left around the bonfire, the figure of a child recalled some question he had asked the guide. She had laughed and said that she did not have the time to deal with it properly as she was meeting her daughter at a nearby cafe. Would he like to come along and join them; she would answer his question then. When they arrived at the cafe, the guide's daughter was waiting for her mother at a table not far from the door. She was not more than seventeen and had her mother's hair which fell in even more generous red curls. After introductions, the guide launched into a thoughtful answer to his question while the girl looked bored and stared at her tea or out of the window, although occasionally Mark caught her throwing a furtive glance in his direction. When he got up to take his leave, she coloured slightly but had said nothing. As he retraced the footsteps of the past, these fragments of memory floated up to the surface of his consciousness.

After lunch, Mark returned to the hotel and found a message from Frau Ornstein, giving the address of Karl Bühler and a telephone number. His call was answered by Frau Bühler and after Mark had explained the reason for his call and the purpose of his visit to Vienna, there was a long pause. She was suspicious and defensive, explaining that her husband was not well and that he would have little to say about his brother's literary career. Mark persisted and gently reassured her that he merely wished to hear a little about the young Bühler which might allow him to understand the author's life better. She agreed reluctantly to a visit next morning but, "for no more than an hour or you will tire my husband too much."

The Bühlers lived in an old apartment block on a narrow street which ran up from the Donau Kanal. Mark threaded the grid of streets south of the Ringstrasse and passed through Arenberg Platz, dominated by the two great flak towers now softened by a covering of ivy. In 1957 he had found these primitive ruins deeply disturbing, pockmarked as they were by bomb fragments and the attentions of Russian machine gunners. Arriving at the apartment, he climbed the stairs to the second floor gripping a conciliatory bunch of flowers and pressed the door bell. Frau Bühler greeted him and, after accepting the flowers, led the way into a small sitting room whose dust caked windows looked out over the street. Karl Bühler was seated in a tall armchair and did not rise to greet him but extended a hand covered in knotted veins. They were a small couple, a little bent and slow of gait, well into their seventies. Karl was nearly bald and wore wire rimmed glasses. The room was crammed with large pieces of antique furniture and dominated by a glass fronted cabinet full of porcelain together with leather bound books. Frau Bühler went out to make the coffee while her husband stared at Mark as he explained the purpose of his visit. He heard his own voice eventually trail away under the silent scrutiny and it was clear that Karl would not speak without his wife being present. Eventually, Frau Bühler entered with a tray laden with cups of coffee and Mark decided to launch into his more detailed questioning.

"Can you tell me a little of your brother's early life, his interests, and perhaps his early writing – as a boy even?"

Karl Bühler took a deep breath and expelled a long sigh. "We lived in Josephstadt here in Vienna, in an apartment, not large, in Piaristengasse. My father was a teacher and a very committed socialist. My mother's family had originally come from Bukovina – my grandparents on that side moved to Vienna in the Eighties. I followed my brother, who was two years older than me, into the Schopenhauer Gymnasium.

"That was a turbulent time in Vienna – politically."

"So you know of 'Bloody July' when the police shot down many workers in front of the Justice Ministry. That had a great effect on my father. He straight away joined the Social Democratic Party and became very involved. My brother too got mixed up in all the doings of the Party – as a lookout and carrying messages and so forth. And then, in the Civil War, father was helping defend the Karl Marx Hof. He was killed instantly by an artillery shell fired directly into the building he was defending. My mother was completely struck down by my father's death and my uncle, Heinz, father's brother, provided all the support we needed in those difficult times." He paused to bring his coffee cup slowly to his lips in trembling hands.

"When did your brother enter University? Can you recall what subject he was studying?" Mark attempted to encourage the flow of reminiscence.

"My brother entered the University the year before father was killed and studied German literature. Uncle Heinz didn't think that it was a very useful sort of education but then he was a businessman. He had inherited an import–export firm with depots in Vienna, Budapest, and Trieste. My brother did start to have pieces published in magazines and so on. Mother was most proud of him."

"And what happened to you when you left school?"

"I hold no interest for you – I am not the poet and author." Frau Bühler coughed and offered Mark a biscuit. "But, as you asked, Uncle Heinz insisted I train in a practical profession and I started an engineering apprenticeship. Then the War started. Uncle was very concerned about my brother being called up and thought that he should stay in here and look after Mother. So he got him a post in the Trade Ministry which was a reserved post – he couldn't be called up. I would have liked a similar protected job although I had teased Otto that he didn't have the stuffing for military life. This must have got back to Uncle who said 'I hear you want to fight for your country – I admire your patriotism' or something like that. So I was called up – sent to the 44th Infantry Division which was soon assigned to the Eastern Front."

"And your brother, did he continue to write? What was his life like here during the War?"

"How should I know!" Karl Bühler's bitterness cut the thick air of the room. "He lived with Mother in the Piaristengasse apartment. He had a girlfriend, Liesl, who he had met at University or with the Party – more I cannot tell you." A long pause again as he sipped noisily from his cup. "I was with the 44th, Deboi was our General, at Stalingrad." He left his sentence hanging as a definite curtailment to any further stories. And then suddenly, "I am also a victim of the camps, other camps – am I not a victim too of *der Hitlerzeit*?"

His wife leaned forward, "Yes – yes. Karl don't shout so. I'm sure that Herr Shilton understands."

Mark waited until Karl Bühler had recovered his composure and then persevered with his line of enquiry, "Did your brother have any friends who still live here in Vienna – anyone who might be able to tell me about the War years and after?"

Karl Bühler looked at the coffee jug, then at Mark, and finally appeared to be trying to discern the titles of the books in the cabinet. He spoke softly with a resigned shrug, "Viktor Herlinger, he was a friend."

"Do you have his address?"

"I might," came the grudging answer and he started to haul himself out of his armchair. His wife staggered forward, grabbed his arm with one hand and retrieved his stick with the other. With her help he shuffled slowly out of the room.

Mark had been so concentrated on his interrogation of Otto's brother and the information, such as it was, that he had hardly noticed Frau Bühler. Now she returned with a more determined gait and sat down opposite Mark as if to establish her presence and to insist on a role in the story. She spoke, almost for the first time, with a pronounced Viennese accent and a voice with a surprisingly youthful lilt. "My husband and I were sweethearts before the War and when he was under orders to go to the East, we got married quickly. He left three days later." She smiled at the memories but her eyes showed regret. "He was taken by the Russians at Stalingrad and kept as a prisoner of war in Siberia. He came back with the last survivors – there weren't many

– in '55. I waited for him for fourteen years – not knowing whether he was dead or alive."

"In 1955!" Mark repeated, shocked at what the intervening years must have meant for both of them. "But he came back – that's wonderful."

"The Karl I married didn't come back," she replied slowly, "another man – utterly changed. We both suffer the War still."

Mark could hear boxes being pulled out from under furniture and papers being shuffled in the room next door. "And did you know Otto Bühler well – or at all?"

"Oh yes, I knew my brother-in-law well. He was always fun to be with although he could also be very serious and intense."

"And did you know his girlfriend?"

"Liesl? Yes, Liesl Schiff was a very pretty, vivacious girl. We often went out as a foursome together, dancing at the Fasching balls." She suddenly reached behind a cushion and produced an old album with faded covers. She turned to a page that held some group photographs, "Look here we are." One photograph showed four young people smiling at the camera in their festive clothes, the men in bow ties and the women with daringly short dresses. "We were so happy then."

Frau Bühler secreted the album again and appeared to be considering whether to speak further. She looked quickly towards the door and lowered her voice, "Otto came under a lot of family pressure to drop Liesl, you understand." It was clear to her from Mark's frown and slight shake of head that he did not.

"Liesl was Jewish and by '38 things had become very difficult for the Jews here – and for their friends. And particularly so for the Bühlers."

"Why for the Bühlers – they weren't Jewish were they?"

"I cannot begin to describe the atmosphere in those times – the new laws, the street gangs, the hate. Frau Bühler's grandmother had been Jewish – her father was a rabbi in Cernowitz. Frau Bühler's parents, the Zeimers, became Christianised and moved to Vienna well before the turn of the century." She did not notice Mark's sharp intake of breath at the name of Zeimer, the narrator in Otto's novel. "But Uncle Heinz got very worried. I remember Karl talking of papers and photographs being burnt – formal denkschrift declarations being sent to the authorities to establish the Bühlers' Aryan status. Uncle Heinz was concerned because he was a member of the Party."

"But the Social Democratic Party ..."

"No, the Nazi Party – Uncle had joined in 1936, to help with business contacts." She paused for a moment, listening to the noises next door. "I don't know any more about Otto. Karl had become estranged from him and I felt that I should be loyal to my husband." She started up towards the door as he shuffled in, lurching towards her with a cardboard box in his hand. He placed it carefully on the small table next to the tray and prised off the lid. It contained a mass of old postcards, business cards and scraps of paper. For some minutes, Karl Bühler silently sifted through these, eventually finding a yellowed card with a printed name and address. He called for his wife to get a pen and paper, and laboriously copied out the details before passing the paper to Mark.

"Herr Viktor Herlinger", he read, "but he lives in Trieste!" Mark had hoped for more helpful information.

Karl Bühler shrugged his shoulders, "That's where he lives – perhaps he comes to Vienna on business at times – you may be in luck."

Mark expressed fulsome thanks for their help and hospitality, and said farewell to the Bühlers. Emerging onto the street he turned right towards the canal and found a workmen's cafe where he ordered a simple lunch of soup with sausage. Peering through the smoke of cheap cigarettes and steam from the tiny kitchen, he found a space at the end of a table occupied by three burly men in heavy work clothes. Opening his notebook and avoiding the gravy and grease on the table, he set down all the information gained during the morning's interviews and was struck, now more forcibly, with the autobiographical nature of the novel. Most first novels contain a rich seam of details from the author's life but he had discovered that the early sections of *'Das Uberleben im Finsternis'* were written so closely to Bühler's life that he wondered whether the later sections might be written from personal experience. The childhood home, the school, and even the narrator's shared name with Bühler's mother's maiden name pointed to a work hovering between fiction and fact. He began to feel a growing admiration and respect for this author who had recounted these exceptional personal experiences in fictional form. He then turned to the piece of paper with Herlinger's address and felt a wave of disappointment. How similar to his experience here thirty years ago, of frustrated research and elusive details. Perhaps there was a slim chance that Herlinger might be in Vienna during the next few days before he was due to return to London. Back at his hotel, Mark rang the Trieste number but there was no reply.

He spent the afternoon trying to persuade the receptionist at the University Library that he was qualified to enter for reference purposes only. The receptionist was polite but firm, adamant that letters were required from London University endorsed by the Vienna University cultural exchange department. Mark retired defeated and depressed by the outcome of his efforts to make contact with Bühler the novelist. Later, in the evening, as he was walking down a narrow ally-like street in the Innenstadt towards his hotel, he passed a basement bar. Thick smells of beer and frying bratwurst were caught by a draught and spiralled upwards to where Mark had paused. He looked about to check his whereabouts in the dying light of the summer's evening. At that instant, the smells, the dusk, together with the memory of the auburn haired girl and the hunters tramping through Breughel's winterscape, all came together to draw up from deep within him the recollections of events of thirty years ago. They had lain undisturbed beneath the accretions of his life until this moment when suddenly they crystallised and re-emerged. He stood motionless as the past crowded in on him.

He had been in a bar one evening in the February of that year with some acquaintances from the University. It might even have been the bar he was standing beside. An hour or so must have passed before he noticed the red haired girl at the other side of the room with a student, probably her boyfriend. Later he looked across at her again. The student had gone and two men, one wearing a cap, the other a felt hat, were talking to the girl. He had thought nothing of it but a while later he suddenly felt a pull at his elbow and the girl appeared at his side. "Take me home now – please now!" she half whispered so urgently that he felt immediately tense and anxiously aware of some atmosphere he did not understand. His acquaintances gave him knowing looks and, shaking his head to disabuse them of their ideas, he followed her out onto the street, as she struggled into her coat and pulled a beret over her unruly hair.

It was bitterly cold and a few flakes of snow were swept down the street. "Quick, down here!" she hissed, pulling him in the direction of a dark, unlit alley. He wanted to ask where they were going and why the need for such haste and secrecy. Urgently, she tugged at his sleeve taking a zigzag route through the Innenstadt maze until they emerged on the Ring Strasse under the baroque facade of the Opera. All the time, she was talking in a low fast monologue which he could barely catch but which seemed about the men in the bar questioning her about her father and her mother's trials and tribulations. By now they had avoided a tram as they crossed the

Ring, skirted Schiller Platz, and set off up Mariahilfe Strasse with the increasingly strong wind behind them. Occasional flurries of snow were illuminated by the street lamps. After a good quarter of a mile during which the girl kept glancing over her shoulder to see if they were being followed, they turned into Kirchen Gasse and he had to trot for a moment to catch up. In the second block, they came to the yawning entrance of an old courtyard apartment building. At that moment, she suddenly stopped, turned to him and just said, "So!" And then, with a little hop, she jumped up and he felt the warmth of her lips brush his for a fraction of a second. There was a thicker flurry of snow and she had gone, running down the dark entrance to the courtyard. He started after her and heard a door slam somewhere. He paused as he entered the inner space; there were hardly any lit windows and the snow was already covering some discarded furniture and machinery with white tarpaulins. Retracing his steps, he had been unable to locate the door through which she had disappeared.

Two men, emerging from the bar, pushed passed him and returned Mark to the present. He smiled at the remembrance of that evening which, still mysterious, was one of many unexpected and random events of that year, reflecting the closed and incomprehensible nature of the city with its shuttered windows, maze like streets, and labyrinthine bureaucracy. Back at the hotel, he decided that it was not too late to try the Trieste connection again and made an international call. Herlinger answered but after Mark had explained the reason for his visit to Vienna, he apologised, saying that he would not be coming to Vienna in the near future. He suggested Mark come and see him in Trieste, "The overnight train is convenient and not too expensive, and I can book you into a good, cheap hotel here for one night." Mark, worried about his dwindling funds, said he would think about it. He checked his remaining money, looked at his return air ticket and then he realised that he was due to call Ruth. As the phone rang in her small flat he felt a sudden, intense wave of longing to be with her. She listened closely to his description of his attempts to unearth details of Bühler's youthful life and how, though his success had been limited, he had discovered the strong autobiographical thread in the novel. He told her about Herlinger who would be able to fill in many gaps and cover the later years but who lived in Trieste.

"But why don't you take up his suggestion and go there for a couple of days?"

"It will be expensive, despite his reassurances, and I don't have any guarantee that his information will be any use."

"Mark, take the chance. He may well be the key to finding out more about Bühler. If you don't go the whole trip will have been – well, not wasted but – not really worthwhile. Do go."

He thought for a moment and then, worrying about the cost of the call, quickly agreed, "OK, – you're right. I just hope Herlinger will come up with something good."

The next evening Mark was at the Südbahnhof station ready to catch the overnight train to Trieste. As soon as the train was announced he set off down the platform. In front of him were a family with two children, Italian he guessed, and the younger, a little girl, pirouetted and danced among the trolleys loaded with luggage. Instantly a giddiness swept over him so that he almost lost his balance. She was Katy at that age and he stared after her as she ran to catch up with her parents. He felt breathless, hollowed out with the husk-like feeling that had become achingly familiar over the years, ever since she had been left as their only consolation. The rupture of their lives had been locked away in some deep chamber of the heart but insistently burst out at off guard moments. Cause and effect, grinding on, left nothing in its path, love destroyed and intimacy sundered. He came to with the shouts of the guard exhorting passengers to board the train and, gripping his overnight bag more tightly, ran to find his carriage.

Three

Early next morning Mark emerged crumpled after a fitful night's sleep in his wagon-lit berth. As he made his way to the city centre, past buildings freighted with the same fruit-heavy swags, the same concourse of historical and mythical figures and heads populating parapets and cornices as lined the imperial boulevards of Vienna. The Adriatic air softened the Hapsburg port, bringing a faint tang of salt and tar on the humid air which moved in gently from the quays of the seafront. Herlinger had booked him a room in a modest hotel opposite the Opera and he then began a tentative exploration of the elusive city infused with the warmth of the languid South.

He had arranged to meet Herlinger at the end of the working day at his apartment on the Via Battisti. He pressed the button by Herlinger's name on the entry phone and, after announcing himself, heard the heavy front door click open. He stepped into a wide hallway with an imposing circular staircase. A voice called from above, "Wilkommen, Wilkommen – stay there Herr

Shilton, I'm coming down". Mark looked up as a sprightly figure descended quickly. His thinning silver hair framed a tanned face and he wore a well cult linen jacket and faded jeans. "It's warm day," he shook Mark's hand vigorously, "My apartment is very airless. Let's go and talk in the gardens." He led the way out into the street.

"So – welcome to Trieste. Have you visited here before? I thought not – we lie a little off the tourist trails here in Italy's appendix, nursing its history on the Balkan shore. And so full of ghosts. Just over there," he gestured across the street towards an intersection, "along the Corso d'Italia, the corpses of the Arch Duke and his wife were ceremoniously borne in 1914." He went on to recount other tales of the city and its inhabitants, Maximillian, Rilke, Joyce, and Svevo.

They had turned left up Via Battisti towards the Karst ridge which still quivered in the late afternoon haze and now entered some gardens shaded by trees with a statue at the entrance. Avoiding a small horde of children rushing out of the dense bushes onto the path, Herlinger found a vacant bench and they sat down grateful for the shade of the chestnuts and cypresses where a small cat stalked some pigeons among the scents of decaying leaves.

"So you have come all this way to discover the soul of Otto Bühler – to translate the essence of his writing – quite a task!"

Mark began tentatively to sketch out the areas of Bühler's life which he was hoping to explore. "I understand you knew Otto Bühler fairly well. I thought it might be helpful to hear about his younger years when he started writing and then to know a little about how he came to write his novel."

Disappointment came almost immediately. "I'm afraid I know nothing of his novel, but we can certainly talk about the young Bühler and maybe a little about his later years. We were roistering students in those halcyon days," and he released a guffaw of laughter, as if at the sheer improbability of such a notion.

"Was he the same age as you?"

"I was one year behind Otto at the Gymnasium but for some reason we became friends – I seem to recall that we met first at the chess club – he was a very crafty player! And it was Otto who encouraged me to join the student section of the Social Democrats. I soon found out why! I got caught up, in a very minor role you understand, in the Schutzbund gun running affair. I would act as a lookout for police or Heimwehr toughs, and maybe carry messages to party Headquarters. Otto was in the thick of it – he used to come up with arms and ammunition from Pressburg on the steamships, bluffing the customs officials."

"And what about his writing – when did that start?"

"He was always writing – sometimes ditties and cheeky little rhymes when he was younger – his school essays were already very precocious – he often got marked down for the romantic pastiche styles he tried out. Then he started writing serious poetry, some of it very political, especially after his father was killed in the Civil War. He got it published first in party journals, newsletters and the like." Herlinger gently tore a leaf from a branch which overhung the bench and smiled, "You know, the odd thing was that he was also brilliant at mathematics. He had a very ordered, precise sort of mind – he used to be pretty short with me when I was vague or indecisive. And yet he was a poet – a strange mixture – people always think of poets as romantic stargazers."

"I believe that he had a girlfriend – Liesl Schiff," Mark drew him back to the main thread of the story.

"Ah so, Liesl – yes, Liesl was lovely – attractive and always laughing. They were a great pair."

"But it didn't last?"

"No. Otto came under great pressure from his family to stop seeing her – she was Jewish. I don't think the Bühlers were a particularly anti-Semitic family, but there was some problem." Herlinger paused and seemed to be searching in the thick shadows among the bushes for some access to the past. "We had some fun then but they were dark times – a growing background of unease – of a threatening future, unknown yet ..."

"So he dropped her?" Mark drew him back.

"One evening, as he was leaving the University, a group of Nazi thugs followed him shouting 'Jew lover' and so on. Otto rounded on them but four of them jumped him and beat him nearly to a pulp."

"And that was the reason he left her?"

"That would be too harsh a judgement – I think he might have stuck to her but Liesl, beautiful Liesl, cared too much for him. She knew about the opposition from his family. She saw the state he was in after the Nazi students had left him lying in a pool of his own blood. She suggested that they stop seeing each other."

"And later – did he never marry?"

"No – not marry, but he did meet another woman – a good woman, such was Otto's luck. She had some minor teaching post at the University – the same time as he was working on his thesis. She had a very strong personality – and striking looking, with red hair, an art historian – he used to call her his Venetian Lady. Grete Taub was just what Otto needed and he moved in with her."

Mark felt a conjunction of details slide together as in a well oiled mechanism. 'Taub' – 'Frau Taub' The missing name of the museum guide he had searched for while standing before Breughel's 'Winter'. "And did they have a child?"

"Yes – a little girl, Ella, born in the early days of the War." Mark hesitated for a moment, wondering whether to air his conjecture that he had met both Frau Taub and her daughter but a sudden sense of reticence prevented him from blurting out this possible connection with Bühler. Herlinger suddenly looked at his watch, "You must excuse me – I have another appointment. But I would be delighted to continue this conversation. Perhaps tomorrow morning – shall we have breakfast at the Caffè degli Sprecchi? – just across the square from your hotel."

"Before you go," Mark interjected quickly, "you might have time to have a quick look at the novel," and delving into his briefcase, he handed over the precious copy.

"I'd be very interested to look through it – very interested. I had no idea that a novel had been published after his death," he flipped through some pages of the book. Then standing up, he grasped Mark's hand with a slight bow and made his way along the curving path until lost to sight beyond a large ornamental urn.

Mark stayed in the cool green air under the trees, trying to assimilate and collate all the details and names which Herlinger had mentioned and to marry them with the story of Bühler provided by Karl and his wife. He needed to bring the information he had gained into some form of cohesion. As he looked through the details he had gleaned from Herlinger and jotted down into his notebook, he was again struck by the close correlation of Bühler's early life with his novel. Indeed the more he compared the novel and the personal history, the clearer it became that Zeimer, the novel's narrator, and the author were one and the same. It even seemed as if Bühler had been at pains to identify himself clearly with his hero by choosing his mother's maiden name and his own schools and addresses. It was true that Zeimer had not broken with his Jewish girlfriend but that remained the exception among the autobiographical detail of the first part of the novel.

Mark mused as to why Bühler had resorted to fiction but surmised that the atmosphere in Austria so soon after the end of the War was not conducive to firsthand accounts of support for Jews. With a small leap of conjecture, Mark was now certain that Bühler had helped his Viennese Jewish friends hide from the authorities. It even occurred to him that Bühler might never have parted from Liesl Schiff but had hidden her and her family. Probably he had been unable to tell his family and friends for the sake of his own and his family's safety. He was not merely a minor member of the pre-War Vienna literati who had written a novel, quickly forgotten. He was one of the unknown heroes of the great tragedy of European Jewry, one of the 'Righteous' whose names should be inscribed in stone; a man who stood out against the mendacity and apathy of his fellow citizens and was not prepared to allow members of that vibrant intellectual community of Vienna disappear to extinction.

By now the light under the enclosing trees in the garden was becoming thicker and the cries of the children fainter as they were shepherded home. Mark too rose, shaking off his reverie. He passed busts half hidden by foliage, memorials of the illustrious exiles and visitors to the city and wondered whether there was a bust of Bühler in Turkenschanz or some other Viennese park. Emerging from the shade of the gardens he set off down towards the quays which were now glistening in the evening sun. Somewhere over the horizon, delineated in gold, lay

Venice among its lagoons. A feeling of euphoria over the unexpected revelations discovered on his trip, engulfed him and buoyed him along the avenues and grand corso which led down towards his hotel.

That night as he lay in bed listening to the sounds of the city, now softer and dying away, Mark experienced a new affinity with Bühler; he had met members of his family and a friend, he had known his lover and, extraordinarily, had met his daughter whose soft lips, thirty years ago, had brushed his own. Whether any of these ideas and emotions would assist him in his task of translation hardly occurred to Mark. He was too enthused by his feeling of proximity to his dead hero, a man he could now respect. A sense of involvement with history and an admiration for the author shone a light on his mundane life and promised a reward of greater relevance to his existence.

Next morning, Mark crossed the piazza to the Caffè degli Specchi and took a seat at a table outside to wait for Herlinger. His light headed optimism had not faded during the night and he smiled to himself glancing around the square bathed in early morning sunlight. The trip to Trieste was proving productive and he stretched out his legs in a mood of relaxed satisfaction.

When Herlinger arrived, he looked tired and the lines under his eyes seemed darker and fleshier than before. He greeted Mark before guiding him by the elbow into the cafe and drawing him to a table half hidden beyond the bar where they ordered a light breakfast.

"Did you manage to have a look at Bühler's novel?"

Herlinger removed the book from the folds of the morning paper he was carrying, "I did – of course, I wasn't able to read the whole book but I skimmed nearly all the chapters and read some sections in a little more detail," he sighed. "You are right; the early chapters are entirely autobiographical."

"And perhaps the rest of the book too?"

"After those early chapters, the story, how shall we say, ceases to be any sort of biography." This was not what Mark had expected but thought that Herlinger perhaps was about to quibble over some details of time or place. Instead, he started to talk about himself.

"At the beginning of the War I was called up and posted to the headquarters of an infantry division. We were sent to Yugoslavia where most of the division's operations were against partisans. I had a fairly easy job as a clerk in the intelligence branch. I used to get a few days leave in Vienna now and then and it must have been in the Spring of '42 when I met up with Otto. He suggested we meet in a decent restaurant – this was before food became a problem – and not one of our old student haunts. He was smartly dressed and had a party badge in his lapel. I whispered, 'Otto, why on earth are you wearing that? You – the fierce socialist – of all people.' He just shrugged and said that to get on in his department one had to join the Nazi party. And he said that Gestapo types visited regularly checking on people's loyalty. He told me that he had been transferred to a special office attached to the railways department of the Transport Ministry."

"But I thought he had a post in the Trade Ministry."

"Well the Trade and Transport had been amalgamated in the mid-twenties and then of course the whole governmental machine had been absorbed into the Reich after the Anschluss. I asked him what sort of work he was doing and he became very animated about the special demands of rail transport in wartime. He was very enthusiastic about his job in the way people are when they discover something at which they have an aptitude. He explained to me the complexities of co-ordinating schedules with trains for troop reinforcements to the East, about whole regiments of panzers rolling to Poland or Ukraine. He worked for a small department known as IVB or something and his boss was a man called Novak, a *Hauptsturmführer* in the SS. He told me how he had to request special trains, *Sonderzüge*, through the Reich Travel Bureau. He had that morning arranged a special transport to Theresienstadt for 'passengers' from the holding camp in Sperlgasse."

"Theresienstadt? In Czechoslovakia?"

Herlinger looked sharply at Mark and held his returning glance. "Yes, the ghetto town and staging post for the camps in Poland and eastward." Mark listened, making the occasional note, barely able to comprehend fully what Herlinger was saying.

"Otto seemed to have distanced himself from everything but the technical requirements of timetabling and obtaining sufficient so called 'passenger wagons'. When

I questioned him to find out what he knew about Theresienstadt, he said it wasn't too bad; that they had a theatre and orchestra, and that the Red Cross visited to ensure that the conditions were good. He went on to talk about the terrible trials of our soldiers on the Eastern Front and the influx of suffering refugees from the East." At last the coffee and food arrived and Herlinger paused briefly in his account.

"I didn't see Otto again until the last year of the War. We were pulling out of Yugoslavia and I was on a liaison trip back to Vienna. We met for a brief chat in a bar. It was as if nothing had changed in the last three years. Otto was still obsessed with the detail of his job and was more than ready to bore me with tales of trains arriving from the East riddled with partisan bullet holes."

"So was he still working in the same department?"

"Yes – and he was absorbed in the problems of interweaving reinforcement trains with others which were travelling West and South to places like Mauthausen as the camps in the East were evacuated in the face of the Russian advance. I tried to get him to be open about who those trains were carrying. He retired behind a screen of details about insufficient special transport being available for evacuation and movement. He saw the need for foot columns from the camps as a failure on his part to provide enough passenger wagons at the right place and time."

Mark paled under the realization of Bühler's role in that vast and terrible industrial system. "But did he really know about the camps?"

"We all knew there were camps for dissidents and Jews where they underwent forced labour. As a staunch socialist, I knew only too well. Luckily I was an insignificant member but many senior figures had been arrested. I remember seeing Jewish families trudging in a column through the streets towards the Nordbahnhof. And there were rumours about death camps and crematoria. In a way, we all knew but didn't face the truth. But he must have known, given his job. He was a part of that system and not totally unwilling."

"But I can't understand – he had Jewish friends, even a Jewish girlfriend."

"I know. It seems unbelievable. Over the years I've tried to understand how he could have come to do that work. There were always two sides to Otto, the warm romantic side and a much more remote analytic aspect. It seems he somehow managed to shut off his more humane side. But I think perhaps there may have been something else. I am sure that he would have done anything for Liesl Schiff – put himself in danger for her, hidden her perhaps. When she broke with him – for the best of motives, because she loved him – he may have felt utterly rejected and that may have influenced him in some way in his attitudes."

"But that hardly seems to justify his complicity in these crimes."

Herlinger paused for a moment, staring at his cup. "I have sometimes wondered about his relationship with Novak. You know – the early, violent death of his father affected Otto deeply. He seemed, so to say, to lack a strong centre. Perhaps Novak provided the guiding figure that Otto sought – and drew him on and down."

"And did you ever see him again?" asked Mark after a few moments silence broken only by the hiss of the coffee machine, his voice hoarse from shock at these revelations.

"Yes. At the end of the War when the Russians had just taken the City. We met for the last time in some scruffy snackbar off Rennweg. He looked terrible – haggard and pale. He said he was suffering from chest pains and was on sick leave from the Ministry."

"What did you reckon – was he really ill?"

"He was certainly paranoid. He told me that most of the senior officials in his department had walked out and that a few days before he went on sick leave, two Jewish men accompanied by a Russian officer had visited his department and questioned some of the staff. But what really worried him was that a colleague had gone into hospital for some very minor operation and died there. He also knew of two officials who had died in suspicious circumstances. One had been found in a ditch after his car had left the road. The other appeared to have hanged himself in his garage but the stool he had stood on was found too far away for him to have kicked it there."

"You say he was paranoid. Were these inventions – fantasies?"

"Probably not. There were at least two Jewish organizations with operations in Vienna who were looking for members of the SS and for Nazi functionaries. Brichah, a Zionist outfit, and also Nokmim, the Avengers, under Abba Kovner who had led the Vilna uprising. They were all hunting down the key figures – and not so key. Many met their deaths."

"How did you come to know all this?" asked Mark, surprised at Herlinger's detailed knowledge of these groups.

"I should have explained. Immediately after the collapse when the Russians entered the City, I just kept out of the way. It was a very chaotic time with Russian soldiers looting and raping from April until the Western Allies arrived in August. Then I got a job as an interpreter with the American CIC, their counter intelligence corps." He paused to give Mark a wry smile. "So you see I'm a translator too. And that is all I know of the last phase of Otto's life. Two years later he was dead. I was still working for the CIC when I saw the announcement of his death in the Neue Presse."

Herlinger took up his pastry and nibbled at it while looking vaguely out of the frosted window of the cafe. He went on to reminisce about the months after the end of the war and how many senior Nazi figures had melted away into the Austrian countryside to lie low. Mark continued to make notes but only in a perfunctory, mechanical way. Herlinger too seemed drained by the effort of recalling the events of over forty years ago. He suddenly pushed away his plate, "Look, I'm sorry if

I have shattered any illusions you may have had about Otto Bühler. He was not an evil man. He got caught up in the machine – and just went along with it all."

"Before you go, do you know of anyone who could help me with the last two years of his life, when he must have written the novel? Frau Taub, for instance."

"I am afraid Grete Taub died some years ago but her daughter Ella, I believe still lives in Vienna. I don't have her address but she used to work for a law firm, Braunhaus...er... Stock und something – she may still be there if you can find it."

They stood on the pavement looking across the piazza. Herlinger turned and shook Mark's hand slowly. "Herr Shilton, it is a novel. Translate it and see it as a tale told by Otto, for whatever reason. We cannot fathom the motives of the dead."

Mark walked slowly down the Piazza Verdi in a trance. The sun by now was well up and the austere official edifices provided no shade. The brightness of the early morning was gone and the sun bore down through a thick haze which deadened the sounds of the city and gathered the heat into the squares and streets. He reached the harbour and crossed the railway lines to the edge of the quay. Here the tracks ran in front of the great civic buildings and the corso. At the height of the Empire, trains would have arrived from all over Central Europe to pass along these quays towards the waiting ships. The horizon was barely discernable as a line between the greys of distant haze and the flat Adriatic. The water had an oily, glutinous quality, burnished by the sun. A boat moved out from the harbour, silent in the heat, and the shouts of boys fishing from a jetty barely carried to where Mark stood.

He realized that he had invested a series of hopes in Bühler, as a brave man who had stood out against a murderous system not only for the love of one young woman but also for all humanity, exemplified at that moment in history by the Jewish community in the city in which he had grown up. Now, brutally, all these thoughts had proven to be mere wishful fantasies. The cold truth was that Bühler had been both weak and compliant. He had known the nature of his job but had hidden from its implications. He was one of many thousand who by their readiness to carry out small but vital functions of the Final Solution had ensured that it proceeded to its merciless conclusion. Mark felt deceived and manipulated by Bühler's text and emptied of any feeling for his role as translator. He was now the amanuensis of an author who both betrayed his fellow man and was a liar. Mark felt his legs almost buckle under him and he sat down heavily on a bollard. It was along these very rail tracks that trains full of Jews had arrived at 'Port of Zion' to board their Lloyd Triestino ships for the promised land and then later, along the same tracks, the lines of crude wagons had delivered thousands of exhausted passengers to their final destination at the Risera de San Sabba and annihilation in its chambers. He wished that he had never come to Trieste and yet with the next thought he realized that without knowledge of the truth he would have been

Bühler's unwitting pawn in a posthumous plan to create a noble persona for posterity. He slowly retraced his steps through the melancholy city towards his hotel to pack and prepare for the journey back to Vienna that night.

On arriving at the station, Mark found the overnight train ready to board and located his wagon-lit compartment. The other five occupants were already in possession of their bunks. They appeared to be businessmen and two were talking in low tones over a supper of pungent sausage and pickled cabbage eaten out of greasy paper. He was forced to climb up onto one of the top bunks and, deciding that reading was impossible in the dim light, lay hoping that sleep would provide relief from the revelations of the morning and from his uncongenial surroundings. Exhausted emotionally, he fell quickly into a deep sleep and was barely aware of the jerk as the train moved off, sliding out of the station and along the coast, past the castles of Miramar and Duino, past history and art.

Mark awoke with a start. He had no idea for how long he had been asleep or where he was in the cloying darkness. Around and below him the unseen sleeping forms were breathing deeply. No sounds came from the train and, feeling no motion, he realized that the train had halted. Then he heard voices on the track outside, whether in Slovenian or nasal southern Austrian dialect he could not quite make out. A clanking and clattering began and then silence again. The carriage gave a sharp jerk and from the opposite bunk came a snort as the occupant turned over in his sleep. For some unknown reason he felt anxiety rising in his throat and the hair on the back of his neck prickle. There came another gentler jerk and the train started moving slowly, the wheels grinding over the rails. The movement was so gentle that it was impossible to tell in which direction the train was travelling. Now fully awake in the stuffy compartment packed with six sweating bodies, he was filled with a growing sense of irrational dread. He lay paralysed on his bunk, totally at the mercy of unknown authorities and functionaries directing the train to whatever destination. He felt the horror of losing all will power, all ability to shape a personal destiny in any small way. As the train gathered speed, he listened to the rising rhythm of the wheels, drumming over the rails, chanting the names, German, Polish, to which the *sonderzuge* had travelled. '*Sobibor, Sobibor*' hammered the wheels. Gradually, by controlling his breathing, he slowed his racing heart and tried to clear away these fantasies. As the train sped north, he eventually fell into an uneasy sleep, hearing the train hurtle into a tunnel which slowly became an endless wooden building, the walls lined with bunks from which emerged arms with outstretched hands, the thin bony fingers almost brushing his face. Jolted awake, he became aware of the dawn filtering around the edges of the blinds.

Four

Back in Vienna, his clothes sticky with overnight sweat and his mouth stale, Mark made his way to his hotel. He had slept only briefly after the nightmares of the journey but, revived by a coffee in the small characterless hotel restaurant, he leafed through the notes from his Trieste research. Had Herlinger revealed all he knew about Bühler? Indeed, the man's detailed knowledge of the darker side of the months after the collapse of the Reich made Mark wonder about his role in the CIC. He tried to curb his imagination as it began to spin increasingly wild surmises.

He wondered if there was any purpose in further research before his plane left the next day. He was almost minded to spend the day sight-seeing or getting drunk in a bar but his recollections of Frau Taub and her Breughel lectures drew him inexorably back to the galleries of the Kunsthistorische Museum. He wandered aimlessly through magnificent halls and corridors encrusted with marble and gilt, past Spanish and Dutch masterpieces, and finally entered the German gallery. It was there, in a corner, that he suddenly saw, not Frau Taub, but what appeared to be her likeness. The plaque revealed it as Dürer's 'Portrait of a Venetian Lady'. Mark realised why Frau Taub had never led her group into this room. She would probably have been too embarrassed by this striking likeness, with its flowing auburn curls and full lips. Mark wondered if her daughter, now older than her mother when he had met her, had flowered into these passionate looks. He decided at that moment to see if he could meet her.

The offices of Braunhaus, Stock, und Westfeld were not far off the Stuben Ring in a baroque building into which an architect had inserted columns of glass and steel. After booking in with his details at the formal reception desk, Mark asked if he could speak to Frau Taub or Bühler, being unsure of her working name. The receptionist confirmed that Frau Taub was one of the firm's lawyers and spoke to her on the telephone. She agreed to come to the lobby to see Mark, who meanwhile sat in one of the large black leather sofas in a state of excitement and anxiety, wondering how he should approach the subject of Bühler's final years with his daughter. After waiting for a quarter of an hour, a woman entered the lobby from the interior door and looked about. She was tall and had long auburn hair, beautifully cut. She was definitely Frau Taub.

"Herr Shilton?" she looked towards him.

"Yes, yes. Thank you so much for agreeing to see me. I wondered if I might ask you about Otto Bühler ..." Mark stopped, realising his approach had been rather inept and was about to continue with an explanation of his role as the translator of her father's novel when he noticed that she was staring at him with a deep frown.

"Nein, nein!" she hissed and, turning, strode out of the lobby, slamming the door behind her. Mark went as if to follow her in a reflexive action of concern but was headed off by the receptionist who had leapt out from behind her desk. Mark shook his head, "Excuse me, do please excuse me," he muttered and, embarrassed and ashamed, quickly left the building. He now realised that it had been a naïve mistake to confront her in this manner at work and that a much more subtle approach had been required. He felt foolish and frustrated. By her reaction, there were events or circumstances in Bühler's relationship with his daughter which still caused a violent reaction forty years later.

Mark returned to his hotel depressed and suddenly weighed down with exhaustion. The whole Vienna trip had been a mistake. He had discovered deeply unpalatable facts and had even managed to upset Bühler's daughter. He let himself into his room and sat morosely on the bed. Opening the mini-bar fridge, he peered at the contents before selecting small bottles of vodka and tonic. The alcohol failed to lift his spirits and as he started to pack his small suitcase the telephone by the bed rang.

"Herr Shilton? This is Frau Ella Taub. I must apologise for my outburst this afternoon. I was unprepared to be questioned about my father after so long – but that is a poor excuse for my rudeness."

Mark sat down on the bed still clutching the drink and juggled the telephone with his other hand. He eagerly accepted her apologies and now explained the purpose of his research.

"Do ask of me all the questions you wish but I fear I may not be able to answer them all."

"I am really looking for details of the last few years of your father's life, when he was writing his novel."

"Really, I can't help much. I hardly knew my father. I was only five years old when he left my mother and myself – and two years later he died."

"Did your mother speak about him to you over the years?"

"Yes – indeed all my so-called memories of my father are stories which Mother told me and which have become part of my childhood story. I should say that in the last years of the War, my parents' relationship was not good and got worse."

"Why was that?"

"At the beginning I believe that they were very much in love but slowly the War changed all that."

"So what was it that caused that change?"

"I'm not certain. The War was a very unsettled time in many ways here in Vienna. And also, they were unmarried, living together, and they had a child – me. Not at all acceptable in our very conservative society.

Well, I remember too that Mother didn't approve of my father's work."

"His writing?"

"No – she was very supportive of his writing. But he had a job in a Ministry, became a Party member, doing some sort of secret work. He did not talk about it." Mark sipped his drink and waited for her to continue.

"Over the years, I've become convinced he was involved in, so to say, the dark side of National Socialist activity. In one way, I wish I knew the truth – imagining is so much worse. I sometimes wonder – would it be better to know?"

Should he tell her what he had discovered in Trieste and would that be better for her? He thought for a moment and failed to come to any conclusion.

"Are you still there?"

"Yes, yes. And you say he left you and your mother two years before he died – why was that?"

"It's a long story. Right at the end of the War, he apparently became very anxious and depressed – more and more difficult to live with. And then there was an incident."

"What sort of incident?" He waited.

"In the summer of '45, when the Russians had arrived, life was very difficult for the Viennese." Another pause "I'm sorry; this is not easy for me." In the silence he pressed the receiver to his ear. Was she still there? Perhaps that was breathing, her soft lips close to the telephone.

"According to Mother, one day my father was followed home by four Russian soldiers. Maybe they wanted his watch or to loot our apartment, I don't know. Anyway, my father burst through the front door closely followed by the soldiers. He brushed past Mother and managed to get away down the rear fire escape. The soldiers then turned their attention to Mother who was protecting me. She quickly pushed me into the kitchen and slammed the door because she feared what might happen." The words came tumbling out now.

"And was she ...?"

"Although I was so small, I can remember to this day, so clearly, the noises. The soldiers were drunk and each took their turn. I must have tried to cover my ears but I couldn't help hearing." Another long pause and then a little breathless, "Mother couldn't forgive my father for his cowardice. Two days later he came to collect some of his belongings while we were out queuing for food. We never saw him again. It must have been in '47 that Mother learnt that he had died."

"And the novel? He wrote a novel in the last two years of his life."

"I'm afraid I don't know about any novel. Mother wanted nothing to do with my father or his memory. She died over twenty years ago of cancer – quite young still –

younger than I am now. Well, I often wonder whether those events had been the cause of her illness."

"Well – maybe."

"You know, both she and I were questioned after the War about my father's activities. I sensed she felt some sort of guilt for what he may have done." Her voice now more remote, "And sometimes I think that I too shoulder some of that guilt – as if it were passed down." And urgently, "Do you understand what I'm saying?"

"Yes, I believe I can understand that feeling." He waited but she had reached the limit of self-probing. "I really am most grateful to you for... well, for recalling these memories – indeed painful memories."

He was about to replace the receiver when she spoke again, more calmly. "Oh – one more thing. I don't know whether this is at all relevant but many years ago, it must have been in the late Fifties, Mother received a letter from an old university friend who had also known my father very well – a Mrs Lisa Kalmar. I found the letter among her papers. She was Jewish and was trying to trace some family possessions – not valuables, I think, just souvenirs – photos and so forth. She had been transported to Theresienstadt and on to a labour camp. At the end she had managed to escape from a so-called 'death march' column. After many adventures she eventually reached America. Her maiden name was Schiff, I seem to remember; yes that was it; Liesl Schiff. The letter came from New Jersey."

"Thank you, thank you so much."

"Good-bye."

He poured himself another vodka and, lying back on the bed, wondered what more he had learnt. Bühler's fear and anxiety appeared to have caused him to leave his family unprotected and brought an end to his worsening relationship with Grete Taub. Of the writing of the novel, however, he still knew nothing. Mark was struck by the irony that Bühler's failure to provide sufficient special transports to evacuate the camps in Poland had necessitated the use of foot columns which gave Liesl Schiff, his first great love, the chance to escape and survive. Digesting all these thoughts, he slowly sat up and continued packing for the next day's flight back to London.

As he stared through the window of the airport bus threading its way through the morning traffic, he vowed never to return to a city so populated by ghosts. The air of gaiety and gemütlichkeit hid too many secrets, too many undercurrents of culpability and guilt. Behind the grand imperial facades, he had sensed layers of duplicity and brutality; a perfidious nostalgia.

Part II

'Translation it is that openeth the window,
to let in the light.'

Translators of the King James Bible

Five

London was crowded and dirty after the wide, clear streets of Vienna. Tired after the journey, Mark unpacked his suitcase and tried to throw off his mood of depression. He set out his notes, together with Bühler's novel, on his desk and tried to assess what his trip had achieved. He concluded that the excursion to Austria had been disastrous. Diverted from his true task of discovering a little of Bühler's background and refreshing his ear once again for the lilt and cadences of the Viennese voice, he had been seduced away onto a detective trail, a Harry Lime in the sewers of the past. He had absorbed little that would be of any help in his translation and had come to despise the author. He was now an accomplice in the novelist's deception with the creation of a false persona whose heroic story hid the horrendous truth; a career of betrayal and of complicity in the perpetration of a great crime. He dreaded the task ahead of him. He was now reduced to the role of a hack translator with no personal commitment to the text. It was too late to abandon the assignment. He had spent the advance and needed the remainder of the fee as he had cut back on his other work. The outlook was bleak. A summer behind dusty windows as a journeyman, converting text, sentence by sentence, as contracted.

Ruth came that evening and cooked supper for them. He joined her in the kitchen, standing behind her with his arm around her as she fried some chops, kissing the warm nape of her neck and memorising the smell of her hair.

Over the meal he recounted the story of his research in Vienna and Trieste, pouring out his distaste for the task ahead. Ruth listened in silence until he had finished.

"So – the 'Good German' turned out to be a 'Bad Austrian'. Are you going to tell Thalia?"

"I don't know. In fact I haven't even started to grapple with that. I've been so focussed on the text and its history."

"I doubt whether Newberg would be very pleased to find that their chosen genius was a Nazi bureaucrat."

Mark played with the remains of the cheese. "There's no real evidence, no documentary proof, for all this. I didn't have to go and uncover all these wretched details. I just want to be shot of the whole business as soon as possible."

"So you don't feel you have to tell them?"

"No. No – I'll just get on and do the job. If there was a need to research his life, it would have been their responsibility." He felt that he had convinced himself even if the tilt of Ruth's eyebrows showed she remained sceptical.

After they had cleared the table and Mark had heard of the latest moves in the complex staff politics of Ruth's school, he started to unroll his old sleeping bag as usual on the sofa. She stopped him gently and drew him into the bedroom. It was the first time they had slept together and he found that, in her arms, his depression and sense of futility ebbed away as he sank into the growing and deepening intensity of their relationship.

The next Tuesday afternoon, Mark made his way to the Senate House where Jeremy Garforth was, as usual, dispensing wisdom. As Mark approached, he found Jeremy in deep discussion with a fair haired young man whose frown showed that he was having difficulty following or at least accepting what his tutor was explaining in such detail. As Mark stood, wondering whether to see what the small canteen in the corner had to offer, Garforth suddenly looked up and recognised him. "Ah Mark! – How's it all going? Just give me a moment or two and I'll be right with you. I just need to set this young man on the right road." He grasped the student's shoulder while giving Mark the faintest of smiles.

Mark had decided to tell no-one, beyond Ruth, about the results of delving into Bühler's past. Such revelations would only complicate any advice he might need about translational problems and could seep back to the publisher with all the subsequent difficulties that would entail. Returning with a tepid cup of tea, he sat down next to Garforth who was gazing after the departing student. "A gifted young man," he shook his head and sighed. Mark merely grinned non-commitally as Garforth continued, "Now tell – your Viennese project – how is it coming along."

Mark began to set out various textual problems he had encountered in the latest section of the novel with which he was grappling. "Hmm ... isn't all translation is an act of re-creation. These decisions which you're having to make, it's delivering your own concept of the original work. Yes, it must be done in a way which honours the author but the result must at the same time have artistic integrity."

"I feel something is getting lost. In the tussle to find the exact word, the perfect phrase, well ..."

"Maybe you should stand back from the text. Allow its underlying patterns to emerge by their own force."

"I'm not sure whether that is more or less difficult if the author is dead."

"Both. He or she is not looking over your shoulder. You're not likely to receive abusive letters from the author complaining about the terrible distortions you have wrought. You know, 'damaging beyond repair the beauty of the original work', are you? But I think some sort of respect for the dead imposes maybe a heavier sense of ... well, of duty."

As Mark made his way through Bloomsbury towards home, he mused on Garforth's advice. He smiled to himself at the irony of such phrases as 'honouring the author' and 'respect for the dead'. His problem was that knowledge of Bühler's past was a corrosive influence on his work of hammering out an English version. It was an influence which he feared would permeate the translation, infecting its character, making it lifeless and flat.

Despite these difficulties and his general dissatisfaction with the whole tenor of his life, the German language provided a haven into which he could withdraw. He had inherited it from his mother and it had infused his earliest memories when her soft whispers of baby talk had been in her own language of childhood. He had been reminded of his earliest encounters with German while visiting his mother at Easter and discovering a battered old photograph album in a cupboard. It was covered with black leatherette and silver writing, its corners bent and frayed. Inside, small black and white photographs had been carefully tucked into adhesive corners. Most had been identified with a place and date in his father's neat handwriting.

On the first page was a group of three laughing figures in a busy city street entitled 'Weimar, April 1934'. It showed his young mother and father and another woman. Mark carefully extracted the photograph from its retaining corners and found an inscription on the back in his mother's careful Germanic script, 'Käthe, David, Hedwig'. Of course, the other woman was his Aunt Käthe, looking so young, and Hedwig was his mother's name although her husband had found it unattractive and always called her Helen. It must have been taken not long after they had met on one of his visits to Germany. Another, 'Erfurt, May 1934' showed a group of men in suits standing before an office or factory in Bauhaus style with his father in the centre, presumably taken on one of his buying trips to an engineering firm. There was a stiff group of his parents and German grandparents in front of their house in Jena, probably on the occasion of their engagement. He was puzzled by a photograph of Aunt Käthe and a man in a double breasted suit and a clipped moustache whom he did not recognize. The inscription on the back revealed him to be Paul, his aunt's first husband who had been killed somewhere in Poland in 1945. In another, 'Jena, September 1938', his mother held a small child, his infant self, in her arms with her parents on either side. This must have been her last visit to her old home. She never again saw her parents who died in a bombing raid in the last year of the War.

A few pages later he found a photograph, 'Coningsby, 1941', of himself, aged about four, with his parents. His father was in RAF uniform and it must have been taken just before he had left for India. Mark remembered his mother telling him how his father had asked her not to bring up the little boy as bilingual. She was disappointed but, as an alien in England, had understood the reason and tried to comply. Over the long months and years of her husband's absence, however, she could not avoid humming the tunes of her homeland in an attempt to console her loneliness. The following pages were filled with pictures of his mother and himself, mostly in their garden in Norwich. She had no contact with her own family and her husband's pointedly ignored her. At first it was just the childish vernacular for Mark's morning milk or his bread and jam on coming back from school. Slowly more and more German crept into their conversations until she had to get him to promise that he would never use German words outside the home. This rule ensured that the young boy revelled in the use of a secret language until, after three years of near isolation, it was all he used at home.

Then a studio photograph on thick card which had been inserted between two pages fell out. It showed him sitting between his parents on a table against which their chairs rested. A date revealed that it was taken shortly after his father's return at the end of the War. Initially he had been appalled to find a German speaking son but soon accepted it as yet another aspect of the new atmosphere of post-War Britain. Mark remembered reading the children's books which his mother had brought from her homeland and by the age of twelve he was totally and confidently bilingual. Just as he was about to close the album and put it away, he noticed a picture of himself with his aunt and uncle taken in 1952 at Waldbröl where he used to spend his teenage summers. He had carefully parted hair, a striped sleeveless pullover and one of his long socks has slipped down to his ankles. His new uncle, Ludwig, stood slightly lopsided due to his damaged leg and they faced the camera stiffly in a garden devoid of shrubs but enclosed by orderly *jäger* fencing.

Mark had a vague and nagging guilty conscience about his mother, who had been widowed now for ten years. He felt that he ought to visit her more frequently and always meant to ring or to write to her more often. Now she had telephoned about his Aunt Mary further reinforcing his guilt. His uncle Morris had died a year previously and Mark had decided not to attend his funeral. He listened to his mother asking if he would go and help his aunt clear out her dead husband's room and dispose of his clothes, a task she could not bring herself to do. Mark agreed reluctantly on the proviso that he could only spare the time to stay one night at his Aunt's.

A week later he found himself in the front room of her detached house, set in a quiet road on the outskirts of the small Lincolnshire town of Market Rasen. Already the covers of uncut moquet exhaled the stale, dusty neatness of an old, single life. In the dining room he found the table still laid for two, the absence of a returning husband from the golf club with his appetite for order and a cooked lunch locking the house in a grief stained stasis.

He listened as she poured out her problems and the difficulties of coping with life on her own. Eventually, she showed him up to his uncle's room, giving Mark some plastic bags and vague instructions about what to do with the clothes. After she had quietly shut the door, Mark crossed the room and looked out of the window. A vista of small, well-maintained gardens met his gaze and despite the sunny afternoon, all were deserted except for a spaniel sniffing a border in the next door garden. The chimes of an ice cream van from a nearby street only emphasised the stifling stillness. The room gave off a hot, dusty odour and, when he opened the wardrobe, this was augmented by the scent of long stale sweat. These soft emanations of his dead uncle gave the room a tomb-like atmosphere and he delayed for some moments before picking out several, nearly identical, grey pin-striped suits and a double-breasted dinner jacket, worn once each year at the Bank's area dinner dance. He checked the pockets which were generally empty except for the occasional bus ticket or paper clip.

After carefully folding the suits and jackets, packing them away into plastic bags, he turned his attention to the chest of drawers. He sorted the shirts and underwear, and began to look through the socks, seeing if any were in good enough condition to offer to the charity shop. At the back of the drawer, he found a slim, brown cardboard box which had been sent through the post; the stamp bore the King's head. Mark opened the box and underneath an official typed letter found some medals. They were mostly in bronze, round or star shapes with multi-coloured ribbons looped loosely through their hasps. One medal lay on top of the others. It was silver in the shape of a cross with a small king's crown at the end of each arm of the cross. It had a white ribbon with a broad stripe of deep purplish blue.

Later, with the bags of clothes removed to the garage to await collection by the charity shop, Mark sat with his aunt in the front room toying with a cup of tea and a small piece of the cake which she had cooked specially for him.

Mark showed her the box of medals, "What do you want me to do with these?"

She peered at the contents of the box as if seeing them for the first time. "I think you should keep them. They're more your sort of thing – you know- being a man. It would be nice to feel they're still in the family. You were his only nephew."

"I don't know anything about medals," he paused to put the medals carefully back into their box and took a sip of tea, "Did he talk much about the War?"

"Hardly at all. He joined up in 1940 and went to Cairo by way of the Cape. I got a few letters from him. Then he was in North Africa and Italy. He ended up in Trieste after VE-Day."

"Trieste," noted Mark, "And did he say what happened to him – you know, between Cairo and Trieste."

"No, nothing really. He just came back and we picked up the pieces of our life again – like everyone else – and got on with living. He went back to his old job at the

Bank and got promoted to manager a few years later." She poured more tea and offered Mark another slice of cake. "He was very content with his life. Whatever had happened in the War was just sort of pushed away to be – well, not forgotten perhaps – but put out of his mind. His only real regret was that we couldn't have children." She hesitated, looking out of the window and listening to the faint early evening noises from the street and surrounding houses. "And a great sadness for me – a very great sadness," and she drew her thin fingers across her eyes.

Next day, Mark travelled south by rail through the hot July countryside towards London. He dozed and woke as the train came gently to a halt somewhere north of Lincoln. He got up, went to the end of the carriage, and opened a window. All was quiet as he gazed at a distant field where short-shadowed cattle stood listlessly in the heat. Then a lark in the high cloudlets above the train began to pour out its liquid song which flowed out over the countryside but remained unanswered from the surrounding hedgerows. Suddenly a dirty orange diesel locomotive hammered past hauling a long line of flats loaded with great corrugated containers. He could barely read the angular logos painted on their sides, names in German and Polish, as the long line pushed on south towards Felixstowe for Rotterdam and then on eastwards perhaps even to Silesia.

After Lincoln, he tried to concentrate and think about his aunt and uncle in their provincial seclusion; the life of a bank manager in a small country town and their still-centred, childless marriage that had somehow endured through the years. How had they sustained hope – and in what? How fended off the nightmare of mortality? Mark, with his back to the engine, fell gently sweating into a reverie, watching the villages and countryside flash past and then recede into the distance, becoming more ordered then remote, before finally disappearing. He dozed fitfully, only awakening as closing walls of blackened moss signalled the imminent arrival at King's Cross.

Back at home, Mark pondered his uncle's medals, turning the silver cross over in his hands and letting the white and purple ribbon run through his fingers. The cross seemed different from the other medals and, intrigued, he looked up the subject in the library. He found that it was a Military Cross which was awarded 'for conspicuous gallantry and devotion to duty'. So Uncle Morris had carried out some significant act as a young officer somewhere in North Africa or Italy. He had never spoken about it, even to his wife, and had clearly never worn the medal or his campaign medals. He had arrived back in Market Rasen in his cheap ill-fitting demob suit and returned to his former life as if the events of the previous five years had been but a dream, or perhaps a nightmare, the memories of which should be carefully filed away and forgotten.

Later, as he sat waiting for Ruth to arrive after her school meeting, it suddenly came to him that his uncle had not forgotten that moment of conspicuous gallantry. It might have been, in one sense, with him every day, underpinning his consciousness of who he was. His realisation that for once, perhaps for only a few precious moments, he had stepped out of that role which most must inhabit as the observers and servants of history and acted. He had acted in some way that had altered the course of events, not in any fundamental way, but significantly. Maybe it was the awareness of his intervention into history that had given him his sense of worth which allowed him then to pursue a life of dutiful, mundane activity until his death. It was this glorious, foolhardy moment of disregard for personal safety that had illuminated his life in a dull little town and a frozen marriage. Suddenly Mark realized that he envied him and he saw his contempt for his Uncle's life as projection of his deep dissatisfaction with his own life; despite his success as a translator, now receiving more commissions than he could handle, the lack of creativity and recognition which he craved caused a constant ache.

Mark now often stood staring out of the windows into the street. It had not rained for some weeks and the pavements were dry and dusty. Already the large leaves of the plane trees looked leathery and yellowing along their edges. Mark watched as a cat inspected rubbish bags in the cramped front garden and noticed a small child dawdling behind its young mother. He turned to make a cup of coffee and wondered how he was going to survive through the summer. With no plans for a break from his London routine or for a holiday, the translation stretched before him as a chore with no relief. The technical problems remained and the Vienna excursion had solved none of them. Instead, it had not only destroyed his enthusiasm but had produced a sense of distaste, almost betrayal, in the translation of what he now knew to be a lie; a deception and a pathetic attempt to whitewash a life, in which any artistic achievement had been overwhelmed by Bühler's connivance with the authorities and their murderous processes.

Ruth was now spending two or three nights a week in the flat and their growing closeness provided Mark with an antidote to any inclination to despair over his work. They shared much in their interests and their approach to life. After long evenings of conversation, he noticed that they both exhibited a certain reticence to share details from their past, despite their deepening physical bond. Eventually it became a tacit understanding that at their age there had been many experiences and relationships but that they both now came together freed from the past, as if young again, illusory as that might be. He knew that any attempt to recount and explain would inevitably alter and even distort their relationship. Far better to begin anew, learning about each other as they found the other, moulded and impressed by experience but without having to accept the freight of each other's history with its failures and pain.

The past, however, has a habit of breaking in to any such clean and clear cut agreement to come together fresh and undamaged. One evening Mark got back late after a meeting in West London and found Ruth already in the kitchen chopping vegetables. "Someone rang for you about an hour ago"

"Uh, uh – any message?"

"No – just said she was Elizabeth."

He felt his stomach tighten and breath catch. He tried to sound unconcerned."Probably a wrong number."

"No – she asked for you by name."

He set up his defences and calmed his voice, "I expect it's from the publishers – an editorial assistant or someone – you know, nagging about deadlines." He hated lying but the alternative would be a whole evening of explanation, a history of half a life; a life which had foundered, threatening his sense of identity, so that he needed to cling to some spar of hope. All this she might interpret or misinterpret and perhaps all would be changed. Ruth continued chopping courgettes. He poured himself a drink and kissed the lobe of an ear.

These little incursions from the past set up small suspicions and queries. A week or so earlier, Mark had met an acquaintance in a lunch time crowd surging down Kingsway. "Mark – how good to see you – how are things?" They chatted for a few moments about critics, reviews and a newly appointed editor. "And I hear that you and Ruth Peters have got together – I knew her at King's." Mark nodded and smiled as the other continued, "That's good – I'm so glad – just what she needs." The remark was left hanging in the air, unelaborated, and Mark was not going to tease out information or gossip from an acquaintance. As they parted, he walked away wondering what Ruth's unspecified needs were and what events in her life had provoked them.

Some weeks later at a social evening at Ruth's school, which he has reluctantly agreed to attend, he fell into conversation with the deputy head teacher, a woman with heavy features and man's hands. "Yes, Ruth was away for nearly a year but has returned much stronger. I'm sure you've been a great help." How could he help her if he knew nothing of her past, a past which their unspoken pact prevented him from probing? In these small seepages, he realized that they had both become aware of each other's pasts but only in vague and unspecific ways.

Increasingly now, as Mark went back and forth over the text, he found minor errors of date or place. He spent some time researching the historical and geographical background, the key events in the Vienna of the Thirties and the town plan of streets and squares. Armed with maps and chronologies, accounts of the literary scene and the city under war in which the protagonists had moved, he found he had to make many editorial corrections to the text, some of which involved further changes. He became concerned that he was stepping beyond the role of translator.

"My dear old thing – all translators are editors as well – and thank goodness for that too." Jeremy Garforth's voice had thickened over the years, Mark noticed, but, when he looked at him sweeping biscuit crumbs off his cardigan, instead of the greying hair and fleshier jowls he saw the younger face from memory of that time when their youthful friendship was forged. Late afternoon sun slanted into the Common Room through the tall windows and the tea lady had long closed her cramped canteen. Only one other occupant remained, dozing over a book in an armchair in a far corner. "Gone are the great days of editors" continued Garforth, in what Mark privately called his pontificating manner, "days when a gifted editor could transform a worthy manuscript with potential into great literature – guiding and mentoring the author."

"But surely there is a limit beyond which the text begins to be the child of two authors."

"Well – sometimes it is just about details, finessing and polishing the raw material. But you know, for some editors it involved rewriting and restructuring the whole text – Gordon Lish's stripping down of Raymond Carver's manuscripts created that marvellous spare minimalism which so engaged Frank Kermode."

"OK – but I'm not an editor developing an author. I'm a translator with some sort of responsibility towards a posthumous text."

Garforth grinned, "I know, I know, but think of the freedom that gives you. A dead Austrian published thirty years ago – what's to stay your hand!" And he let out one of his characteristic guffaws which jerked the sleeping reader back to consciousness.

Six

Early August and London was hot and already tired of summer. Troops of bored and exhausted tourists filled the pavements. On a humid afternoon with the threat of a thundery shower, Mark made his way down Exhibition Road after an hour's research in the Goethe Institute. Children were massed around the entrance to the Science Museum and the steady line of traffic gave off clouds of dust and fumes. The air became darker and thicker as he turned into the Cromwell Road. A few large drops of rain fell and then suddenly he was caught in a heavy downpour. He noticed that he was near the entrance to the Victoria and Albert Museum and, running up the steps, pushed into the lobby through a small crowd that was shaking the rain from hats and umbrellas. The rain increased in strength until the drops danced off the pavement and he turned into the interior of the museum. He glanced idly at a pillar to his right which carried a simple plaque. 'To the memory of those killed in the World War 1939-1945' it proclaimed and below were a dozen or so names, the men's with just one initial but the women's with Christian names. It was not clear whether they had been killed abroad or by a bomb while on duty at the museum. At least Uncle Morris had survived and returned home to his dull job sustained by his moment of glory.

Mark turned back to the open doorway where the rain was lessening as abruptly as it had started. Already a weak ray of sunlight filtered through the ragged edge of the thundercloud. Suddenly, the scene was illuminated by a burst of light turning the wet steps to a shining silver and beneath the plane trees by the street patterns of gold flickered across the paving stones. Momentarily, the traffic thinned and he stood at the top of the steps entranced by the facets of reflected light. An image of the silver medal came to him as he paused, transfixed by the scene before him. A jumble of mental shapes slowly but inexorably slid together as in a Chinese puzzle of interlocking pieces which defy order but then, in a moment of inspiration, form one whole perfectly. He knew what he must do. His translation must let in the light, the light of truth, albeit metaphorical. Not the actual events of Bühler's wartime work but a deeper truth about his evasion and self deception, and what that had meant for the lives of so many. His honest translation would illumine his own life too; it would be his contribution to a righteous history and give his work meaning and value. As he walked slowly down the steps to the street below, he realized that by transposing the roles of Resch and Zeimer in the text, he could provide a meaningful indictment of Bühler's actions while still preserving the structure of the novel. As he made his way past the Oratory, he felt a strange combination of elation and deep calm which he sensed would lift his depression over the task and give a new purpose to his humdrum life.

———𝓥———

Back in the flat, Mark pondered whether to reveal his plan to Ruth. It was possible that she might try and dissuade him and at this early stage he did not want to be forced to provide rational arguments to support his deeply held, intuitive conviction that this was the way forward. He did not consider the practicalities and details of his plan, deciding to keep silent and to reveal the result when completed or at least well launched.

That evening Ruth announced that the lease on her flat was coming to an end shortly. "I've been looking around, mainly at adverts, but the sort of thing I need just hasn't appeared." Mark wondered why Ruth, at her stage in life, was still living in furnished flats for only a few months or a year at a time. There seemed to be some impulse to keep on the move or at least not to commit to any longer term arrangement. He had not wanted to enquire into the reasons for her peripatetic life in case it breached their mutual assumption that the past was to be left unexplained.

"Why don't you come and stay here – just while you're searching for a new flat?" He hoped his voice did not betray his neediness and the hope that they could live together, at least for a while.

"It would only be for a week or so, not much longer. Would it be a terrible nuisance?"

"Of course not. You are usually here for two or so nights a week – it wouldn't make much difference. And I'd like you to stay." He reached out and held her shoulder, returning her grin, and then took her in his arms, feeling her slight body mould against his responding to his urgency.

So Ruth moved in and for a few days there were suitcases, boxes, and bags of her belongings stacked in the hallway but these were soon distributed around the rooms, into cupboards and wardrobes. At first he had to suppress a vague feeling of resentment as his orderly existence was disrupted. Bottles of cosmetics crowded the bathroom shelf and she reorganized cupboards in his cramped kitchen. He soon forgot any misgivings about the new arrangement and relaxed in the knowledge that she would arrive every evening and that their lives were becoming ever more inextricably entwined. They became more familiar and comfortable with each other, learning quirks and dislikes, taking account of each other's way of living.

He lived in her presence, savouring stolen glimpses of her as she peered into the bathroom mirror, a towel slipping from her narrow hips. The new physicality of their life together, attenuated his sense of loss and isolation. He remained unwilling to heed the future, when she might move on, or to dwell on the time before they met with its loneliness and the burden of guilt. Sometimes he realized that this was an artificial existence and that inevitably past and future would have to be accounted for. One night as she lay in his arms and he wondered what would become of them, he found his chest wet with her silent tears. Later she turned over and slept. In the morning, no explanation was offered or sought.

Mark set about changing Bühler's text. It appeared an essentially simple matter of interchanging the two principal characters so that it was Resch who evades discovery and survives while Zeimer betrays the hidden family and eventually takes his own life. He had already translated about two thirds of the original text so with notional scissors and paste he chopped and transposed sections, changing names and attempting to gloss over any resultant cracks or ragged edges. After several days hard work it became apparent that the initial plan was not as simple to implement as he had expected. The major changes created ripples which spread throughout the text. What seemed at first to be small adjustments spawned an alarming domino effect which set off other chains of altered circumstances and details.

By early September he realised that he was committed to a fundamental rewrite of the book. Ruth noticed that his depression had lifted and that he was working longer hours at his desk. Although he was concerned both at the scale of the task to which he had committed himself and at the risk he was taking, he felt lighter and clearer about the way ahead. If at any time he sensed a foreboding about the possibilities of discovery and how he would argue his case, he thrust these anxieties aside to be met when he had completed his plan. He knew that it was unlikely that his translation would be checked in detail against an obscure, out-of-print original. He would deal with Gillian Marshall and her boss when the time came.

Meanwhile, he settled into the companionable routines of life with Ruth so that soon chores were shared and habits meshed together to mutual convenience. On wet Sunday afternoons, they would leave the newspapers scattered on the floor amid the mugs of cold coffee and retire to the bedroom. Later Ruth would gently explore his body, noting the thin scar on the upper side of a wrist that stretched across two blue veins or let her fingers search around the knob of bone on his elbow, the result of an old fracture. These tender investigations of clues to past events were left unresolved. As he caressed her, Mark wondered about her past affairs, how many there had been and whose hands had moved over her angular body before his. Did she too speculate about his previous lovers?

Occasionally, leaflets from estate agents would arrive through the post for Ruth. He hoped that nothing suitable would catch her eye and that she would eventually give up looking for somewhere else. If only she would stay permanently, perhaps they could build a life together which would allow him, perhaps allow both, to come to terms with whatever flotsam they towed behind them. He started reading the discarded leaflets, looking for two or even three bedroom flats to which, in his fantasies, they might move and live happily ever after.

A few weeks later, Mark had almost completed the new translation of *Das Uberleben im Finsternis*. He had inserted new details into the preliminary chapters so that Zeimer's life followed that of Bühler's even more exactly. He added an additional threat to Zeimer because of his Jewish ancestry. When questioned by the Gestapo, he agrees to betray not only the Jewish family whom he is hiding but also his widowed mother. Mark was not sure about this last insertion but his contempt for Bühler overcame any scruples or literary judgement. Departing further from the original, he has Zeimer failing to commit suicide despite a determined attempt. He is eventually reconciled with Resch who has returned from Switzerland. He finally leaves Vienna and teaches in a country school. Remembering the postmark on the manuscript, Mark sites the school near Bad Ischl.

Although the rewritten novel had a good level of structural integrity with which Mark was well satisfied, it had a fundamental flaw. It was written in English, sounding as such, and he knew only too well that translations have a very particular tonal quality. This gives a clue to their origins and each language, translated into English, has its own timbre. He had always tried, while writing in clear, lucid English, to transmit a feeling for the cadences of the original language. He had to admit to himself that his new text lacked the Germanic rhythms and over-elaborate syntax of the original which at the start of the project he had been at such pains to reflect. The whole purpose of his visit to Vienna, the wish somehow to find the voice of the dead author, had been to that end. His enthusiasm in changing the plot had overwhelmed his judgement as a translator. If the inserted scenarios did not betray the changes he had wrought on the original, the lack of an underlying oddness of the prose, the hallmark of translation, would certainly do so. For some days he was in despair, unable to work or even look through the pages of his new version. Some deep instinct still prevented him from sharing his doubts with Ruth and he wrestled with them alone.

Autumn was eager to arrive and as Mark returned home one evening, the wind hurled spatters of rain with the first falling leaves against his body as he trudged along wet pavements. Street lights illuminated puddles and the windscreens of passing cars. He realised that he had to find a way out of the impasse but shied away from the inevitable conclusion. He turned the key in the door of the flat, climbed the stairs, and still in his dripping coat, surveyed the papers on his desk. He finally admitted that if he was to pursue this plan to a successful conclusion he must write the novel again, this time as Bühler in his native Viennese tongue. The subsequent translation should, at that final stage, not be too time consuming. As he poured himself a glass of wine from yesterday's bottle, he realized that he had to become Bühler. Not the false Bühler of the original but the man true to himself whose self deceptions had been scoured away. All this would take time and he was already perilously close to the deadline he had agreed with Gillian Marshall. He decided he would get up early, before dawn maybe, and work for two or three hours before the business of the day started.

And so, as the days drifted into October, Mark began again. Very early, he would gently slip out of bed without disturbing Ruth and sit at his desk sipping strong coffee. In the still darkness he inhabited Bühler, in the upper room of some country gasthaus, and wrote in the lilting rhythms of Vienna which now flowed as if he had never left the city but had been born there. His imaginative, creative urge, so long stifled by his translation work, was released as he created the new character of Zeimer. As he wrote on, morning after morning, he found himself a battlefield of conflicting emotions. In assuming Bühler's persona, he became increasingly sympathetic to his history, understanding him in the political and social milieu of that time, empathy eventually threatening to overwhelm his contempt for the novelist and his deception. Yet the more he had become the literary reincarnation of Bühler, the more he came to despise his alter ego's duplicity. These opposing sentiments created an element of self hate which began to infect his role as amanuensis.

One morning after two hours of writing he suddenly noticed the sunlight slanting across his desk. He looked up to see the yellow light percolating through the remaining leaves on the plane trees in a parody of early spring. For days now there had been a late Indian summer, a miraculous time of light and warmth but tinged with regret that these were the last precious days before the cold harbingers of winter. It was too enticing to remain indoors so Mark decided to set off for Highgate Woods. The narrow paths were still fringed with green undergrowth and the calm was only punctuated by birdsong. He found a small clearing and, throwing down his jacket, lay staring up through the leaves as the dappled sunlight shifted about him. Relaxed for the first time for weeks, he listened to the distant shouts of children running playfully through the wood.

As he half dozed, he remembered the *indianers,* they were red Indians, chasing through the slopes of the Waldchen under the tall columns and fan vaulting of the beech trees. Stripped to the waist, a crow's feather stuck into a bandana, and faces patterned with charcoal, they would surprise hiking couples or swoop down on other children. Those teenage summers spent at Waldbröl with Auntie Käthe and Uncle Ludwig, with all the freedom of the woods and hills; Heinz his chum, Julius the butt of their jokes and horseplay, Jurgen, and the other boys from the town. How Jurgen, a year older than the rest, became their leader. What did he call their group? Yes, the *Waldshar,* the Forest Band. And they had a base in some sort of workings up near the top of one of the hills covered in the great beech trees. A quarry or maybe an old earthwork left over from the War. It had a kind of small chamber entered through a stone doorway – you had to stoop. Damp inside and some rubbish, a rusty metal box with army markings and full of what seemed used bandages. 'Our *Schloss*', the group had called it but Jurgen had said 'No – it's the *Bunker*' and no-one argued because he was older and had them parading, shirts off, so that he could feel their biceps and Julius, who was dark and small – he had an Italian mother – always got laughed at because he was a bit weedy. Mark remembered he was much in awe of Jurgen who had been in the *Deutsches Jungvolk* for a couple of years towards the end of the War. Mark had asked if he had any badges or insignia as he collected those sort of things but Jurgen said that his father had burnt them all. Why? Because they belonged to the previous time – that was all finished now, everything was new and different his father had said.

Mark felt the breeze send small flurries of seeds floating down from the branches above as he ran his fingers through the leaf litter at his side. The sun was momentarily hidden by a cloud as his memories drifted on to a long forgotten, darker recollection. The group had been gathered outside the Bunker one hot afternoon and Jurgen had ordered Julius into that dark little chamber for some failure or other. They heard the sounds of an argument and then Julius pleading for him to stop and then a strangled cry. Mark had looked at Heinz for a long moment and both made just the beginnings of a move towards the doorway but no more and then looked away. He remembered that they could not meet each other's glance.

The next summer everything was different. Jurgen had been apprenticed to a stone mason in Waldbröl and was working on reconstruction projects in Cologne. The group did not reform and Julius was not around – Heinz would not say why. Eventually, in answer to his questions, Auntie Käthe explained that Julius had 'taken his life'. Mark was initially puzzled by this phrase, wondering in what direction he had taken his life, until she explained that he had gone missing last winter and was eventually found by the *forstmeister* hanging from a beech tree.

Although the writing proceeded faster than he had expected, Mark became aware of the deep disturbances his dual role of author and accuser was creating. Frequently now, he awoke some time after midnight shivering in sweat soaked pyjamas which clung to his body so that he had to slip out of bed, towel himself down, and change. Lying awake in the damp sheets but hoping to sleep before dawn, he wondered whether he had taken on an insuperable task. He was worried too about the deadline for submission of the translation and this stress, coupled with exhaustion from lack of sleep, began to affect his relationship with Ruth. He became increasingly irritable or would lapse into long silences. Too often he fell asleep in his chair after supper and only woke to become aware of Ruth switching off the television and preparing for bed. She was puzzled by his overworked condition as he had claimed to have reduced his other translating commitments. Mark had been careful to hide his rewriting from her and still felt that the time was not right to reveal his plan to her. He wanted more than ever to show her the completed work and induct her into its secrets when honed and polished.

At the end of November, Gillian Marshall rang for the second time to enquire when the translation would be submitted. Mark had just finished the task of recasting the original and was now feverishly translating it into English. He was slowed down by other commitments as he had to maintain his contacts with other publishers. Christmas was already looming, with his mother's requests to join her and his cousins for the festival. Ruth had spent two weekends away and their lives seemed less joined under the effect of Mark's strain and her end of term work load. As the year slid to a close, he realized that their life together had somehow drifted into the stasis and mutual near indifference of a relationship which had lost its impetus. He desperately hoped that the coming year and the submission of the translation would allow them to come together and recreate the light, easy companionship they had enjoyed in the summer.

After Christmas, Mark returned to the flat to find it cold and unwelcoming. Ruth was still staying with her parents until the end of the holiday period and the street was deserted, riven by cold, dusty winds. He pulled on an old cardigan over his jersey and grimly sat down to complete the translation. After the weekend, Ruth returned, relieved to be free of her demanding parents and he felt calmer now that the end of his project was in sight. He had managed to reassure Marshall that he had nearly finished and although she complained about how difficult it had been to persuade Aubrey that Mark would eventually deliver, she accepted his excuses and they agreed a date for him to bring in the completed work. Towards the end of the month, he completed the fifth and final read through of the translation. Although there were still some aspects of the language which he was not entirely happy about, he knew that there was nothing more which he could do. The restructured novel fitted its separate parts together perfectly, with fewer inconsistencies than in Bühler's original. It flowed seamlessly and gave no indication of being dismembered and recast.

"So here it is at last." Marshall gave a slight snort and rolled her eyes up to the ceiling. Her office was even more crammed with papers and boxes full of files. Noticing his surprised glance, she explained, "We are moving to some frightfully smart, state-of-the-art offices in Victoria. Aubrey says Bloomsbury is finished and we have to embrace the Twentieth Century, let alone prepare for the next! Anyway – 'Hidden in the Shadows' is finally translated?"

"OK – I'm sorry it didn't make the deadline – but perfection takes time," he countered, half ironically.

"Well – no harm in the end – Aubrey has decided to reschedule it for the Spring list and we have the cover ready to go – the text design won't take long."

"And proof reading?"

"Yes – and Aubrey wants Gail Bisset to have a quick look at it." Mark's breath caught. Bisset might just spot the changes if she was conscientious but he had resolved to face up to these threats.

"And how's young Helmut? Any more gems discovered in publishers' cupboards in the East?" he tried to sound off hand but he needed to know every source of danger.

"Helmut? He decided to take a break from publishing and go travelling. He went off to India – we got a postcard from him – he's staying in an ashram somewhere." She started to cast about in her desk drawers and peer into nearby boxes. "I know it's here somewhere but we are in a bit of a state with the dreaded move coming up."

Next morning he slept late, slowly surfacing as a period of intense dreaming ebbed away. The deep painful layers left him, just for a moment, with a curious but strong physical impression of Jamie's little arms held tightly around his neck. As the sensation faded, he found that tears were rolling down his cheeks as he lay staring at the ceiling, forming little pools of salt water in the whorls of his ears.

Seven

One evening he decided to tell Ruth about the rewriting of Bühler's novel. He had to admit that he was anxious about her reaction despite a certain pride in his achievement and hoped he would revel in her amazement and praise.

When the time came, over supper, she was certainly amazed. He had not thought how to explain his motivation to her and had blurted out the facts.

"Mark, you are pulling my leg aren't you?"

"No, I'm serious, utterly serious. I had to put the record straight or at least to indicate a truth about Bühler."

"But quite apart from the ethics of changing a posthumous text – even by a little Nazi like Bühler – you will be finished professionally when it all comes out."

"It won't 'all come out' as you put it. Who'll notice the changes? There is hardly a copy of the original left.

Gillian Marshal can't read German and just wants to get the damned book published."

"You are being impossibly naïve – you will almost certainly be found out. Then what'll happen? Professionally, you'll be finished."

"What do you mean 'finished'?"

"None of your publishers will ever touch you again. You'll never get another commission – you'll be left to tutor thick school children at cheap crammers – what a career prospect. I don't think you have begun to realize what you have done." Flushed, she picked up her glass and went into the kitchen where she started to wash up pans, banging them into the sink.

Mark did not move but sat staring at the crumbs on his plate. His world had just flipped over like a tossed coin and he was now staring at the reverse of all his plans and hopes. How could he not have seen all this, he asked himself desperately. How could he have thought that rewriting the novel was any sort of noble riposte to Bühler's deception? He trembled to think of the public and private humiliations of discovery. Far from giving meaning to his life, his pathetic attempt to rewrite history, as he imagined, would now destroy his career, leaving his life in ruins. He sat on, unseeing and almost unable to comprehend his changed world until he felt her hands on his shoulders. "Come on, you old thing – maybe something can be salvaged from the wreckage – don't despair.

Mark slept fitfully that night and woke at dawn with a sensation of dread that tightened and soured his stomach. In the days which followed he went through his routine of painstaking translation as an automaton. He felt permanently sick with apprehension and dislocated from the world, his senses dulled, with his impending nemesis for ever present at the front of his mind.

When a telephone call came from Professor Bisset, it was as the confirmation of his worst fears. She had seen the original text and he knew that Thalia had asked her to look at his translation. Trying to remain calm and relaxed, he heard her ask him to come and talk to her in her office in UCL about something that had come up. This enigmatic message left him with no clear clue as to the purpose of the meeting and whether he was to be unmasked.

Bisset had a brisk manner and penetrating eyes framed by thick rimmed glasses. Her office, encroached by bookcases, had a distinct orderliness despite piles of box files and a corkboard covered with post-it notes above her desk. She made him a mug of instant coffee, fussing over the electric kettle in the corner and apologising for the lack of biscuits.

"Mark, thanks for coming in for a chat. I just want to try out some ideas on you." He still felt unable to relax in the face of these enigmatic remarks, anxiety gripping his entrails. "I've been thinking about the area you work in and looking at some of your translations." She paused to return to the corner of the room to hunt for a jar of sugar. Mark felt any icy wave of dread spread up through his chest and stifle his breathing. "I'm beginning to plan a two day conference," she continued, "with a general theme of German literature in the thirties but perhaps as a particular response to fascism." He speculated whether this was some kind of diversion. "And I just wondered if you could give a paper on the inter-War literature of Austria and the German speaking East – I haven't got the terms right yet and we'll need some snappy title which will intrigue people enough to bring them in – and pay their registration fee, I might say!" she gave a quick girlish giggle. He was not yet ready to lower his guard but the purpose of the meeting did not appear to be the announcement that she had discovered his deception. They talked over the scope of the paper which he might prepare and about the academics whom Bisset was planning to invite. Mark agreed that on receipt of an outline of the conference programme, he would submit a general synopsis of a paper he might contribute.

As their discussion drew to a close, he felt he had to know for certain whether she had noticed any changes to Bühler's original plot. Without that knowledge, his fears and imaginings would haunt him through the months ahead. "So you liked Bühler's novel – an unusual plot given its time?"

"Yes, yes – I did like it. Well worth republishing in English."

He noted her non-committal enthusiasm and determined to probe harder, "And did you feel the translation did it justice – it's so hard to be objective oneself."

"Yes – I thought you'd done a good job, Mark."

"And you felt it managed to maintain a Viennese flavour – that sort of Austrian character?"

Bisset did not answer immediately but looked thoughtfully at the pile of papers on her desk and then at Mark. "You don't know how fortunate you are working outside academia. OK, it's got its uncertainties but you are not subject to the pressures of university departmental life. I'm head of department now, we are short of two staff members, I have to plan a completely new course for next year, and on top of all this, the research assessment exercise is a complete nightmare. The department just hasn't managed to publish enough this last year." She turned to look out of the window to where pigeons wheeled about the neoclassical pediments and he wondered where this outburst was leading. "Yes – I did look at Bühler's novel over a weekend away in Suffolk. I skimmed it and it looked interesting. I told Thalia that it was worth republishing in translation." She stared into her coffee mug. "Then just recently, I'm sent a photocopy of the original, a proof copy of your translation and a ridiculously short deadline for comments just at the moment we are all preparing exam papers. I had a quick look at your translation, Mark. I thought it good – yes, very well done. But I wasn't going to do a critical analysis as if it were a first year student's work, sentence by sentence. I told Thalia as much – or at least hinted so." He suddenly felt the room lighten and the air clearer. He now knew for certain that she had not spotted the changes and that Thalia was unaware of his plan to tell the truth about Bühler.

Slowly the sense of dread faded over the next few days and yet the gnawing sense of a damocletian threat hovering somewhere above still remained. He hoped that this too would gradually disappear but he had to acknowledge that, when the review copies were sent, out some expert in Austrian literature who had read the original might detect the plot changes. He became quieter and more introspective, and in response to Ruth's repeated questions about how he felt about the possibility of discovery he was noncommittal despite his fears. His initial confidence and moral certainty over what he had done had ebbed away. He acknowledged not only Ruth's warnings over the dangers of his course of action but the thin justification for his whole project. After a couple of weeks he finally realised that he had to take some action or be a paralyzed victim of events beyond his control. Perhaps there was still a chance to abandon his attempt to reveal Bühler's deception and remove the threats to his future career and livelihood. He might be able to intercept the publishing process and make some excuse, yet to be invented, to Thalia.

After summoning up his courage, he rang a copy editor to avoid speaking to Gillian Marshall and asked how the book was progressing. She rang back after checking with Production to report that it had been swiftly typeset, the cover had been prepared in advance and it had been sent to the printer some days previously. He managed to elicit the name of the printing firm and rang off regretting that he had not taken action earlier and intercepted the manuscript in some way while still at Thalia.

"The book is already at the printers."

"What! That was quick." Ruth paused for a moment, "It might just be worth seeing how far the printers have got with it. It could be just sitting there before they have done anything."

Mark left very early next morning for Havant where the printing firm was situated on a large industrial estate. He took the first stopping train to Southampton which ground its way through a thick February fog, barely hiding the warehouses and scruffy back gardens of Battersea and Wandsworth. As the woods and suburbs of Surrey emerged in the morning light, hope and anxiety churned in his chest. He became more optimistic as the fog cleared to reveal the frost covered fields of Hampshire. He caught a taxi to the industrial estate and arrived at the printing firm's building as the receptionist was unlocking the main door. He eventually met an assistant who, presuming that Mark came from Thalia, took him through into the warehouse section of the building. He pointed to three pallets covered in plastic wrapping. "There's the consignment, one thousand five hundred copies of 'Hidden in the Shadows'. OK? Usual delivery arrangements?"

Mark nodded and stared at the dozens of neat boxes as a chill spread up from his feet. He realised that he had reached the end of any attempt to avert the possibility of disaster. On the journey back to London, the rhythmic swaying of the carriage and the drumming of the rails drew him on inexorably to his fate. Yet by the time the train had slowed through Vauxhall, a hint of bravado grew over him. As the architect of his destiny, he would see this business through whatever its outcome. For a moment the old euphoria of his concept for rewriting the novel resurfaced as a counterweight to his apprehension about the future. That evening Ruth sensed his ambivalent mood and, wrapping her long pale arms around him, gazed at him with wide eyes and an infectious grin. Laughing, he felt all his concerns evaporate at least for that moment and returned her kisses.

The book launch was to be held in an independent bookshop not far from the British Museum and Mark managed to persuade Ruth to come with him. He needed her support to face the team from Thalia and the representatives from the big bookselling chains in case his rewriting of the plot was unmasked, provoking instant and very public humiliation. Gillian Marshall met them at the door complaining about the small number of guests who had bothered to attend, much to his relief. Grasping a glass of wine and juggling a canapé, he looked round the room and noticed Jeremy Garforth in deep conversation with a young man who was leaning against the poetry section bookcase. Then Marshall introduced him to a Frau Grünheim from the Austrian

Cultural Institute who wanted to talk about Bühler's place in the Viennese literary scene. She admitted not to have read the original as the Institute's library did not have a copy. She expressed surprise that a book with this particular plot could have been published in 1955. Mark muttered something about the innovative commissioning policy of Wallisch Verlag. He was saved further probing by Aubrey clearing his throat and tapping importantly on his glass. He made a short speech welcoming everyone to the event and went on to give a brief literary biography of Otto Bühler. He did not dwell too long on the complexities of the plot and Mark received the briefest, albeit congratulatory, mention as the translator. To Mark's surprise he then asked Frau Grünheim to say a few words. She spoke a little about Buhler's earlier work and then began to discuss his motivation for writing the novel. "We can tell from the earlier chapters that there is very strong autobiographical element in this work of fiction. But what makes it so intriguing is the confessional nature of the main plot. We are left to speculate whether the author was indeed the actor in the events of his time which he describes or whether this is a more general exploration of national guilt and possible atonement. We shall never know but it certainly provides a dramatically new perspective for English readers on this talented Austrian author." She concluded with an overview of the novel, a plug for her Institute, and some final comments, "'Hidden in the Shadows' provides a link, at least at a critical level, with the German literary movement, known as *'Gruppe 47'*, and it is a welcome addition to *Trümmerliteratur*, the literature of the ruins of the Third Reich."

Mark, who had been holding his breath during much of her talk, slowly relaxed. She had been sailing close to the wind but had expressed exactly the view of Bühler which Mark had risked so much to articulate. He eagerly took another glass of wine from a passing tray and basked in the success of his plan. Any threats had evaporated and only now could he glance back to the hours of grinding work and the deep cost to his sanity. Later, Garforth pushed his way through the crowd. "Hey, Mark, I've been asked to write a review of the Bühler novel by the TLS. Can we meet up? It would be helpful to have a chat before I start scribbling?" Mark, still relieved and even elated by Frau Grünheim's insights, agreed, with the realization that he could handle any sparring with his old friend and mentor. The guests did not linger and Mark managed to draw Ruth away from a bookseller with whom she was chatting. As they were leaving, Marshall asked him if he would return the copy of *'Das Uberleben im Finsternis'* for their archive. He managed to mutter that he would hand it back as soon as possible. They escaped into a cold March wind which swept down the street and found a nearby Greek restaurant for supper.

Over the mezze, Mark wondered, "What do you think I should do about the copy of the original?"

"There's a real danger there," Ruth replied thoughtfully, "you've got to avoid that – could you, well, lose it somehow?"

Mark could not help laughing, "You're really getting into the whole conspiracy, aren't you! Yes I suppose I could – say, leave it on a train."

"Yes – but not actually leave it on a train. Just use that as an excuse. You really need to dump it so that it can't resurface."

Later, Mark tested out various scenarios in his mind for the disposal of the original. He eventually chose a plan which appealed to his romantic imagination and avoided any cold blooded destruction of a book which would be anathema to him. Indeed, it needed to be sacrificed with all due care and reverence by consigning it to the waves so that it would be carried out to the limitless sea. One evening, after attending a literary festival at the South Bank, he started to cross the Hungerford footbridge, having taken the book with him. It was late and the last civil servants from Whitehall had already crossed the bridge to catch their commuter trains home. The city lights were reflected in the long puddles which made progress along the walkway into an obstacle course. A keen wind was blowing and the beggar who usually played a penny whistle in the little alcove halfway along the bridge had decided to go to wherever he spent his nights. Mark stopped there and opened his briefcase.

He carefully wrapped Bühler's novel in a copy of the Evening Standard and looked both ways along the footbridge. It was quite deserted but he stood motionless for a moment as a late train rumbled across the railway bridge behind him, shafts of light from the carriages illuminating the ironwork of the bridge. In the silence which followed, he stepped forward and threw the bundle out into the darkness. He watched it fall towards the foaming water beneath. For a moment it was illuminated by a random shaft of light as the book broke loose from it wrapping and the pages spread and fluttered. Then it hit the water and to his horror was swept under the bridge upstream on the roaring flood tide. He had not noticed the direction of the torrent below and now the book was being carried up past Westminster. In his fevered imagination, he saw it floating on up to Chelsea where it would be found at dawn on a brick strewn shore by a dog-walking editor who would return it safely to Thalia. Alive to every fantasy, every variation of exposure, he trudged homeward and arrived dishevelled and depressed. Ruth only laughed, ridiculed his fears, and made him a large mug of cocoa.

He now had to confess to Gillian Marshall that he had lost the book. Mark was not a practiced liar and dreaded having to deliver his concocted story convincingly without stammering or blushing. He made an appointment and discovered that Thalia had already moved to their new offices. He found Marshall in the corner of a bright, noisy open-plan office. Crates full of files and books were stacked around the desks. He sat down and avoiding her eyes, faltered through a rambling explanation about a late evening seminar at a suburban college, falling asleep on the train, and waking to find his briefcase containing the book had been stolen. He managed to counter her questions about reporting the incident to the police and the reason for taking the book that evening in a manner which seemed to satisfy her more readily than his mumbled explanations convinced himself. She sighed regretfully, "Well, I suppose it can't be helped. It's a pity – it was the only copy we could lay our hands on. Thankfully Helmut photocopied it." He suddenly remembered Professor Bisset mentioning a copy and he should have guessed that one would have been needed. "I think Bisset returned it but where the hell it's got to in this chaos I haven't a clue," and she gestured to the half empty crates stacked about her. "Aubrey insisted on creating a new archive section so it may be there or even ended up in non-fiction for all I know."

That evening, he felt more relaxed and self-confident than for many months. All his anxieties had left and he could begin to think gently about the coming spring and his life with Ruth. His meeting with Garforth would provide a further opportunity to broaden the reception of the recast novel and a truth about its author in a review. They met in a dusty restaurant in Marchmont Street where Jeremy was greeted as a regular and valued diner. He praised the cheap Barollo as 'the blushing Hippocrene' and deconstructed the menu almost in a parody of the self he had created and carefully nurtured for decades. Over the saltimbocca he quizzed Mark about Bühler's early literary career and the autobiographical nature of the novel. Mark steered him towards considering the confessional element in the work and hinted that there might be a deep source of guilt which drove the narrative. Jeremy looked thoughtful as he scribbled notes and then looked at Mark, "And how much editorial work did you have to do while translating?"

"A bit – you know, places and times which didn't quite tie up."

"Anything more fundamental?"

"Fundamental? Well, a translation has to be honest, has to reflect the truth, don't you think?"

"Yes, I'd agree with that. So you think that Bühler was trying to say something about Austrian anti-Semitism in general – even his own culpability?"

"Who can tell what the author was trying to say – we only have his text."

"I can see you're not going to give me any more leads, are you. But that's all very helpful – thanks for those markers – I'll be able to get something useful together by next week."

Now that the crisis appeared to have receded, he felt closer to Ruth as they spent more time together. In the early evenings he found himself listening with a new intensity for the first tiny sounds of her key in the front door lock. He was aware of gazing at her long, delicate fingers as she gripped her biro when correcting a pile of essays or ran her hands through her short, cropped hair. Some mornings when he woke, calmer now, he paused to watch her sleeping face and her slightly quivering eyelashes before he slipped out of bed to make their early morning tea. Slowly, but inexorably, he felt more at one with her and only completely and fully himself in her company. Despite her reserved manner and long silences, he sensed that she had come to depend on him more, often asking for his views or ideas, especially about the complexities of staff politics at her school. So as the trees outside the tall windows extended their buds and broke softly into leaf, he experienced an resurgence of spirit that might allow the recent events, and the long, dark past, to fall away in the face of a future which held the promise of sunnier uplands.

When he read Garforth's review in the TLS a fortnight later, he was encouraged to note that it perceptively probed and speculated about Bühler's motives in writing such an apparently confessional novel. These intuitions were matched in a short review of foreign novels in translation in the Guardian's Saturday Review. Mark at last felt justified in seeing through his remoulding of the plot from that damascene moment on the Cromwell Road, through all the agonies of re-writing, and then the tortures of self-doubt. His task was completed and Bühler's lie had been translated into truth.

Mark suggested to Ruth that they get away out of London during half-term as a friend of his had offered his cottage on the Pembrokeshire coast. The small coastguard's building was damp and smelling of mould on their arrival and although the stove in the little living room began to dry out the rooms, a stiff sea breeze pressed rain through the edges of the ill-fitting windows. The following days saw sun alternating with flying cloud and the weather became warmer. The double bed was large and soft so that they lay late into the mornings, entwined and listening to the sighing of the wind through the branches of the gnarled plum tree outside the window. They walked along the cliff tops, ate ravenously and drank in a nearby pub. Once on a walk, as he crawled to peer over the cliff edge to see the seal pups mewing below, she gripped his coat tightly, her laughter tinged with real anxiety.

As their cares and concerns dropped away, they allowed themselves increasingly intimate conversations and even their silences were shared with a growing feeling of contentment. Mark dared to allow himself to wonder, if barely to hope, that this might be the beginning of a new life for him with Ruth; a shared life with limitless potential. Whether she reciprocated these same hopes remained obscure. He had become accustomed to her reticence and inhibition against giving full expression to her emotions. Even after all these months she remained an enigma and yet that was also her attraction, the unknowable which fuelled his desire. In a moment of clarity it came to him that his doubts and yearning, the fragile hope and insistent foreboding, were the very fabric of life lived at the edge, lived fully and with a total engagement that rejected that sedative which masqueraded as happiness.

Mark had become, if not complacent about the success of his subterfuge, at least comfortable with the diminishing likelihood of discovery, despite a deep undertow of uncertainty. He felt proud that he had not become party to a false picture of Bühler's life and had stood out for truth, albeit a metaphorical truth. Yet there were moments when he was back in those dark days of October, the black autumnal hours before dawn, being Bühler and taking on his persona and style of writing so that the story would flow seamlessly. Back then he had at times felt he understood him and even in the exhaustion of rewriting, experienced a kind of empathy.

At times during that week away on a wild coast, as he stood staring out over a grey sea and felt the wind tearing at his clothes and wrenching at the leafless thorn hedges, he wondered whether he would have acted differently from Bühler had he been in the same circumstances. But the more he thought, the more his ideas followed an unending circular path. If he had been in those same circumstances, he would indeed have been Bühler and not a professional translator with self-righteous moralistic notions. At least, Mark insisted to himself, he would not have written a false testimony. Whatever his actions, he would have owned and lived with them. Bühler had died even before his self-justification had been published. He must have died content, or at least in hope, that history would judge him by his posthumous novel. Mark had thus been denied the possibility of exposing him and his literary lie. He had, in some part, failed in his quest to bring Bühler before the court of wider opinion but there were moments when he felt that his altered translation was underhand, an easy blow against one who could never respond. He consoled himself that many a biographer had indulged in character assassination and that it was not he who had chosen a dead author as his subject. He felt cheated that the author had escaped retribution and even at some moments anger that the hidden message in the altered text would reach only a few readers who would recognise Bühler in Zeimer and know him for what he was.

Part III

'Tell me what you think about translation and I will tell you who you are.'

Martin Heidegger

Eight

It was in early July that the envelope arrived. Mark turned it over as he ate a solitary lunch in the flat, looking for clues. It came with a Thalia Press franking mark and he wondered what the envelope might reveal. He had remained alert over the months to the possibility of discovery, so each small event which originated from the publishing world caused him a frisson of anxiety. More optimistically, he wondered if the envelope might contain an invitation to undertake a new project or even news of some success, some prize for translation. He wiped the butter from his knife and slit the envelope open. Peering inside he found a second, smaller envelope addressed to him at Thalia in neat, spidery handwriting. He opened it and took out a single sheet of lined paper which bore no address but a date.

'Dear Mr Shilton,

I have read your translation of 'Das Uberleben im Finsternis' which I found very interesting. I would be most honoured if you would agree to meet me. I can be found at the Cafe Mozart in Swains Lane every Tuesday afternoon. I do hope that we shall meet.

Yours respectfully,

Erik Eckstein'

Mark read the letter again and considered it with a translator's eye. The handwriting copperplate but with italic modifications, suggested an older, well educated writer. The style of English did not flow naturally and he guessed that the letter was not written in the author's mother tongue, a conclusion reinforced by his name and it spelling. The letter gave no address to which a reply might be sent and he mused as to the purpose of the letter and its writer's true intentions. He put the letter back into its envelope and pushed it into the drawer of his desk. He had no wish to meet Mr Eckstein and felt a vague sense of danger which he dismissed as anxious imagination.

During the next two weeks, Mark occasionally thought of Eckstein's letter but felt no inclination to make a decision. On a Monday evening, when Ruth was at a late staff meeting with school governors, he came across the letter while searching for a pencil in a drawer and reread it. He realised that until he met the writer of the letter, it would remain a source of irritation and concern.

The next day, Mark made his way to Highgate and walked along Swain's Lane looking for the cafe. After he had strolled downhill some way, the lane turned west into an area of modest suburban houses. In a row of shops and restaurants on the right of the road and beyond a broad pavement he found Cafe Mozart, with an awning and some tables and chairs set out in the afternoon sun. He entered blinking in the cool shadow after the glare of the street. The cafe was only half full and it took him some time to scan the various tables set around the walls. Most were occupied by couples or lone women and there was no sign of anyone who might be a Mr Eckstein. He took a table by the window and decided to wait while he had a coffee. He was warmed by the sunlight slanting through the window and decided to relax and enjoy the break from routine even if no meeting materialised. The half opened glass door of the cafe reflected the part of the pavement which was otherwise invisible from his position and yet allowed him to scan further down the lane. He idly watched passers-by intersect in and through the reflections of the glass, inspecting each for the unknown foreigner. He had fallen into a reverie when an old man, slightly stooped, entered carrying a plastic bag and made his way directly to a table at the rear of the room. Mark decided that this had to be his correspondent or he would abandon the attempt. He approached the table.

"Mr Eckstein?" The man looked up with a start and stared at him over his reading glasses. "I'm Mark Shilton – you wrote suggesting we meet."

The man's eyes widened and his narrow mouth spread into a slight smile, "Of course, of course. I am most delighted to meet you. Do please sit down. Will you have a drink, perhaps a coffee?" Mark sat down and gestured to a waitress to take an order. He noted that Eckstein had a strong accent, probably German with a hint of an Austrian lilt. He would have to listen more to be certain.

"And perhaps you will join me in trying the cafe's excellent *zwetschen fleckerln*?" added Eckstein. Mark was now able to observe him more closely. He was probably in his mid-seventies, balding, and with a taut finely lined face and a deeply cleft chin. He had slightly sallow complexion which might have been his natural colouring or a summer tan. Although his jacket, with a plain shirt and tie, had a greasy patina of long use, he dressed neatly and had short deft movements of his hands. Mark's coffee and the plum pastries arrived and there was a moment's strained silence before they started eating.

"The *fleckerln* are really very good here. I could not invite you to a discussion without trying them." Mark wondered what sort of discussion might develop. Perhaps Eckstein was a member of a reading group and wanted privileged access to the translator. "I much enjoyed your translation. It reminded me very much of the Vienna of those days."

"So you have lived in Vienna?"

"Oh yes – I was born there though I left before the War. And when I was a student, I used to read anything new being published – there was such a lively literary scene."

"And did you, perhaps, know Otto Bühler?"

"Not personally, though I knew of him. I was not in his circle of literary types although we were at the University at about the same time. He was always with a crowd of Social Democrat students and some rather pretty girls. I left Vienna after I graduated, not very brilliantly I must confess. I was fortunate to find a position out in the country. Very rural. At Bad Aussee."

"I believe Bühler had poems and short pieces published while he was still a student."

"Yes, he did and I was a great reader of his work then – I still am." And he grinned with a slight sideways glance at Mark, as he pulled at a long hairy earlobe. "I enjoyed those novels of the years before the First War by Roth and Zweig." They discussed the Viennese literary scene between the Wars and its cultural context for some while. Eckstein appeared very knowledgeable and provided some telling insights into the way Bühler's style developed. He eventually brought the conversation back to *Das Uberleben im Finsternis*. "But Bühler's novel is very interesting. Quite remarkable, for its time."

"I agree – I hope you enjoyed it." Mark was content for Eckstein to lead the conversation towards whatever goal he had in mind.

"Yes, of course, and, if I might say so, a most accomplished translation. It is strange to see one's own language transposed into another tongue. It gives an altered perspective." He reached down and ferreted about in a worn plastic bag by his chair and produced the reviews from the TLS and Guardian, roughly torn and heavily annotated in biro. "Indeed, a significant and noteworthy translation."

"As a translator, one has certain editorial responsibilities as well." Mark observed in as neutral a manner as he could muster. "Especially with a text published posthumously a considerable time after the author's death."

"I quite agree." Eckstein accepted in a serious tone. "Indeed it seems there may be structural changes required in order to deliver a text suitable to its new audience." So Eckstein had probably read the original and compared the two versions. "One can only speculate about Bühler's motives for writing about this subject so soon after the end of the War. So – more coffee, Mr Shilton?"

"No thank you – I must be going soon." Mark felt that he was not fully in control of the discussion and was now concerned as to where it might lead. "But it's been a pleasure to meet you."

As he asked for the bill at the counter, he turned for a moment and saw Eckstein rummage in his bag again and slide a well thumbed copy of the original novel onto the table. After waiting for his change he turned to find that Eckstein had disappeared. Mark looked briefly round the cafe and then went quickly out onto the street.

As he emerged into the sunlight looking each way up the lane, he thought he saw a figure in a hat turning the bend of the lane to his left.

Mark now realised that the meeting had been left in a thoroughly unsatisfactory state and that too many questions remained unanswered. He needed to know what more Eckstein knew of Bühler and more importantly whether he would take any action over his detection of major changes to the text. Without this knowledge, he would be left in the same agony of uncertainty that he had suffered months ago. He strode quickly in the same direction and as he reached the straighter, uphill section of the lane, he could see the same figure walking fast, almost trotting, past Highgate Cemetery gates. A few moments later, amazed at the ease with which the older man was maintaining his lead, Mark looked up the lane just in time to see him turn into Waterlow Park.

By the time Mark reached the entrance, which was momentarily blocked by a group of young mothers with prams, there was no sign of the fugitive. He walked towards the centre of the little park and scanned the lawns and paths curving between shrubs and flower beds. A figure which might possibly have been his quarry could be seen for an instant through the furthest trees and bushes. He ran, sweating in the heat of the afternoon, and eventually emerged panting onto Highgate Hill. There was no sign of Eckstein on the pavements now thronged with children walking home from school. He gave up the chase feeling frustrated and foolish. He had missed an opportunity to bring this episode to closure and it would nag him for months. A bus was coming down the hill picking up speed after a stop and he suddenly noticed Eckstein sitting by a lower window. Although he did not turn his head, Mark had the distinct impression that he knew his pursuer was on the opposite side of the road, staring at him.

As Mark's glance followed the bus down the hill and he noticed that below him, silhouetted against the dusty afternoon sunlight, was the hospital. It was there, long ago but ever present, after the doctors had done all they could and Jamie had finally lost his battle, that he and Elizabeth had emerged into the thin light of that dawn. Both were exhausted, weightless husks, utterly emptied of any expressible emotion and so frozen with grief that he could not even reach out for her hand. That was when the wall between them had started building.

Mark recounted the afternoon's meeting and subsequent chase to Ruth that evening. She was intrigued and questioned him about Eckstein's view of the novel. "It must be gratifying for an author to meet one of his readers," she concluded.

"'Translator' you mean."

"In your case 'author'," she countered, "do you think he had compared the two versions?"

"I think he must have but I'm not sure that he fully realises the extent of the rewriting."

"Will you go and meet him again?"

"No. I think that might be dangerous. I don't think he will get in touch again and if he tries to expose my rewrite to Thalia, I'll bluff my way out of that if it happens." He tried to sound confident but remained unconvinced.

To an extent, Mark forgot about his encounter in the Cafe Mozart and was absorbed in his busy and varied programme of seminars and translation work. Occasionally he wondered what Eckstein was up to and whether he was poring over the two versions of the novel. It was now July and the weather became hotter and more humid. Despite the noise of traffic, they slept with the window wide open to draw in the night breeze. He found himself dreaming more vividly during these warm nights; images and emotions which lingered on waking until they seeped away out of his consciousness during the morning. Vienna increasingly featured in these dreams, drawing on memories of his student days, mixing and juxtaposing people and incidents in a seemingly random fashion. Sometimes his recent return to the city provided new material for the tapestry of tales woven by his dreaming.

Nine

The weather continued sultry and heavy. One night, it must have been a little after midnight, he was woken by a great crash of thunder and which wrenched him upright. He listened for the sounds of the storm but the night was soft and quiet. For once, the noise of traffic had drained away and even Ruth's breathing was hardly audible. Then the dream came back to him. He was sitting at a table in a Viennese cafe. As often, the venue was an amalgam of cafes he remembered but with the tables and chairs of Cafe Mozart. Frau Ornstein and Viktor Herlinger were chatting at the table and suddenly Eckstein joined them. He ordered his favourite plum pastries and after they arrived pushed the plate across to Mark encouraging him to eat. After cutting the pastry carefully with a fork, Mark looked up and noticed that Eckstein had been replaced by a young man whom he recognised from the old photograph. It was Otto Bühler. At that moment Mark had been wrenched from sleep and found himself sitting on the edge of the bed, trembling slightly.

The proposition that Erik Eckstein was Otto Bühler hovered tantalisingly at the margins of his mind. He shook his head in disbelief and quietly got up and went out of the bedroom. The idea seemed absurd but, as he sat at his desk staring out at the street lighting filtering through the leaves of the plane trees, he started to gather together the pieces of a jig-saw. There was very little evidence and what could be gleaned was vague and circumstantial. Eckstein had an original copy of the novel and was fond of *fleckerln*. Had not Frau Ornstein remembered his love of the plum pastries? Such tiny scraps of clues. Eckstein had left Vienna for a job in the country at Bad Aussee and the 'posthumous' manuscript had been posted from Bad Ischl. Mark rummaged in a box file of memorabilia and found a map of Austria which was disintegrating along its folds. He searched the area south of Salzburg and noticed that Bad Aussee and Bad Ischl were only a few kilometres apart. The name of a nearby village, Altaussee, caught his eye and triggered some memory. He found his notebook in which he had scribbled information during his trip to Vienna and Trieste. He was sure that Herlinger had said something about the SS planning a last stand after the fall of the Reich which was linked to escape routes for wanted officials. There, in his distracted scrawl after the terrible disillusionment of that meeting in Trieste, he had jotted down 'Altaussee'. He also remembered he had seen a photograph of the young Bühler. He rummaged in the box file and found a poor photocopy of the image. It was difficult to see any resemblance between the young man and Eckstein although Mark wondered whether he could just detect the shadow of a cleft chin.

This was a thin collection of mere hints which proved nothing. Eckstein had left Austria before the War so the hypothesis that Bühler might have faked his death and managed to get to London was impossible. Mark returned to bed, confused and wondering why this strange idea had wrenched him out of a deep sleep. In the morning, he said nothing to Ruth and decided to let the matter rest.

During the next few days, the dream and its implication resurfaced only to be firmly repressed. Mark concluded that it was a fantastical idea with no sound evidence to support it and was a product of his underlying anxiety about what he had done to Bühler's novel. A week later, he was musing over a cup of mid-morning coffee when he remembered Eckstein shooting him a quizzical glance when he recounted how he had been at university with Bühler, as if testing his reaction. Now Mark found he could not shake off this vague intuition that Bühler might have resurrected himself however irrational such an idea might be. Mark looked back at the entries in his notebook and wondered how reliable an informant Herlinger might have been. He appeared to have known Bühler well and had been ready to provide the detail of Bühler's wartime work in the Ministry. Herlinger himself had a complex history, working in intelligence during the War and then as a translator for American intelligence.

He realised that he had made the assumption that Eckstein's assertion that he had left Austria before the War might be false and perhaps Herlinger had put him in touch with the people in Altaussee who arranged his death certificate and escape to London after the fall of the Reich. Mark cast these inventions aside and returned to his work. During the day, his hypothesis appeared quite ridiculous and he even wondered whether he was losing his grip on reality. In a moment of openness, he poured out his idea to Ruth and although she was initially intrigued she agreed that it was an unlikely story. But sometimes at night his suspicions would re-emerge in the darkness and refuse to be so easily dismissed.

One day Mark found himself flicking idly though the telephone directory and discovered a dozen Ecksteins living in London. Four of these had addresses in North London and he wondered which belonged to the enigmatic figure he had met in Cafe Mozart. Later, he returned to the directory and tried to work out which Eckstein lived closest to the cafe. This proved a fruitless exercise as all the addresses were within a couple of miles of Swain's Lane. He could not rid himself of the notion that Eckstein might be Bühler. Once lodged in his mind, the suspicion refused to be eliminated and continually edged into his consciousness, a distracting nervous tic which plagued him in the early hours of the morning.

Finally, he realized that his theory had to be somehow put to the test. He must find Eckstein and question him further, perhaps even confront him. For three successive Tuesday afternoons he sat waiting for Eckstein in the Cafe Mozart, ordering another coffee every hour. His quarry never entered the cafe and the staff, on being questioned by Mark, could not remember the old gentleman. He decided to telephone the four Ecksteins. His first call was answered by a woman. When he asked to speak to Mr Eckstein there was a pause and she told him that he had passed away a year ago and enquired as to the reason for the call. Mark mumbled a hurried excuse and put the receiver down sharply. He could not face repeating this direct approach and resolved to try a more oblique line of enquiry. The second address on his list was in Hampstead, in a street off Pilgrims' Lane. Next morning he set off and found the house was a double fronted Victorian villa with wisteria over the door. Impressive wrought iron gates shut off the paved driveway occupied by a large BMW. This was clearly not the home of the Eckstein he had met, thus another candidate was eliminated.

The next address was in Finsbury Park and Mark set off by bus, skirting the Heath, and on through Tufnell Park. Fonthill Road had seen better days. Tall late Victorian villas had been divided into three or more flats. Dustbins spilled onto the pavement and were patrolled by feral cats. He found the address led to a basement flat with paint peeling from the front door. A tired net curtain was drawn across the bay window which let onto a litter strewn space below street level. He rang the bell and waited. No sound came from behind the door and he rang the bell twice more. As he was standing wondering what to do next a woman carrying a clutch of plastic shopping bags appeared at the top of the stone steps above him.

"Oh, hello. I'm looking for Mr Eckstein. Does he live here?"

"That's right, love. Mr Eckstein's lived down there for years."

"He doesn't seem to be at home. Have you any idea when he might return?"

"'Fraid not, love." She sat down heavily, arranging the bags carefully around her. "Known Erik for years, I have, since I was a kid. Me dad used to look after him specially just after he arrived. You see he was a DP, you know, homeless after the War. He comes and goes, you never know when. You might find him down at the station. Spends a lot of time there. Bit of a train spotter." And she gave what sounded like a snigger.

Mark thanked her and returned to street level. He guessed that she had meant Finsbury Park station and he had a rough idea where it was. He set off in what he hoped was the right direction, wondering whether this would be another fruitless stage in the search for Eckstein. If the woman's memory was correct, Eckstein had arrived after the War as displaced person. More light was thrown on the shifting perception of the man. Finding his guess was correct, he entered the station subway and climbed the stairs to Platform 5. The station was almost deserted. An air of boredom wrapped the only two travellers waiting patiently on benches watching the pigeons pacing back and forth. There was no sign of Eckstein even when Mark strolled along the platform to peer beyond the waiting room and lavatory block. The rails began to emit a hissing sound and suddenly an express hurled itself into view as it accelerated northwards from Kings Cross. As it roared passed on the central rails, the sound was redoubled as a similar train came from the other direction, not yet slowing as it headed for the terminus. The travellers gripped their bags more tightly and the pigeons whirled up above the station buildings. In a moment, the two trains parted leaving only dying reverberations of their passage.

As the circling pigeons swooped down again, he suddenly noticed a figure sitting on a bench on the far platform. It was a man who had not been there before but had been revealed by the departure of the intervening trains. He was stooped over something he was reading and annotating. The figure could be Eckstein, thought Mark, and he quickly ran down the steps to the underpass. Ignoring signs to the Underground, he found the stairs to Platform 1. As he emerged into the sunlight again, he walked carefully to the left of the station buildings so that he would not be seen by the figure on the bench. Mark stopped at the corner of the building and observed that it was probably Eckstein. As he approached softly, he became more certain that he had reached the end of his search. He stopped, watching as Eckstein carefully wrote in the heavy book on his knees, and then slowly moved up behind the bench. He had been so focussed on the chase that he had not thought of what to say to him and suddenly blurted out, "Otto Bühler!" He saw Eckstein stiffen with a jolt and his head jerk up. He turned and saw Mark.

"Ah, Mr Shilton, I wondered if we might meet again. I take it this is not a chance encounter." Mark stepped forward and, moving a plastic bag of what seemed

Eckstein's lunch, sat down next to him on the bench. "So you want to talk more about Herr Bühler."

"Yes... well that is ... I believe you are Otto Bühler."

Eckstein returned his look coolly, "That is quite absurd. Bühler is dead these forty years, my dear sir. True, I did know him back in Austria but all that was a long time ago."

"Perhaps Bühler didn't die," countered Mark, "I have discovered certain evidence that leads me to believe that you may be Otto Bühler."

Eckstein gave a barely audible snort and turned to Mark with an ironical smile, "And what might be the nature of this so-called evidence, may I ask?"

Mark was not going to reveal the sparse evidence for his theory. "I've just been to Vienna and I spoke to your old editor, Frau Ornstein – and to your brother Karl."

Eckstein appeared unimpressed. "Who is this Frau Ornstein? And Bühler's brother was killed in the War."

"No, Karl Bühler eventually returned from a Soviet prisoner of war camp. But I also met Viktor Herlinger in Trieste who was very interesting on the subject of Otto Bühler."

Eckstein's head jerked round and he stared intently at Mark. "So you spoke to Herlinger – and what did he tell you about Bühler?" Mark realized that he had scored a direct hit and that he should not reveal the results of his research at this stage. It would be better if Eckstein was unaware of the extent of his knowledge. "He told me about your wartime work in the Ministry of Transport."

Eckstein opened his mouth to speak but at the same moment another high speed express train hurtled passed, only a few feet from where they sat, the noise and rush of air forcing them into silence. As the train receded into the distance, Eckstein looked at him intently again. His mouth seemed smaller and his eyes had narrowed. "These are ridiculous allegations – I refute them absolutely. But let me tell you Mr Shilton – if you were to go to the authorities with this mad theory of yours, I would reveal how you have changed Bühler's novel in your so-called translation. I have a copy of the original. I know how you have altered and twisted the plot. If I bring your deceit to the notice of your publisher and to the world – oh yes, I know of your standing as a translator – your career will be over, you will be ruined. Mr Shilton, we are bound together in a bond of silence. Neither of us can pass on what we know or, in your case, claim to know."

Mark reeled back away from Eckstein. He had not expected such a violent reaction, indeed he had not thought ahead as to how he would respond to the challenge which fed his deepest fears. The description of their mutual bond of silence was crude but true. His vehemence, however, supported Mark's suspicions despite his denials. He pressed on, "So admit that you are Bühler!" Eckstein declined to answer and sat staring across to the next platform, playing nervously with his pencil.

"And why, Mr Shilton, did you alter the plot? What possible reason did you have for this act of desecration?"

Mark decided that at least he would tell the truth. "I learnt of your work in the transport section of IVb, how you arranged the trains that left Vienna for Theresienstadt and onwards for the camps. And later on the evacuation to Mauthausen. Your novel showed the Zeimer-Bühler character in such a different light – a completely different story with its autobiographical suggestions. By changing the plot, I gave a truer picture of the sort of person you are – not an actual description of your activities but a deeper truth within the structure of the novel."

He did not reply immediately. They were wrapped in a silence which came cocooned by the mid-day heat and bounded by the cooing of pigeons and the faint rhythm of traffic below the station. When he spoke it was with a quieter, tired voice. "I did meet Bühler after the War. As you know, I had a clerical post in the stadtamt at Bad Aussee and often took my lunch in the gasthaus in the town square. One day I saw Bühler across the gaststube bent over a bowl of soup and when he had finished his meagre lunch I went over to him. He had some sort of part-time teaching job locally and was staying in Altaussee. He looked rather ill and seemed very low. We chatted briefly and he told me he was doing some writing when he felt up to it. He seemed very bitter, talking about how he had been forced to renounce love and to work as a bureaucrat to support his mother." Eckstein fell silent for a while and just as Mark was about to question him further, he continued. "I only saw him once more, again in that dark gaststube, and he looked a lot worse. I felt he was on the edge of some sort of physical and mental breakdown. I enquired after his writing and he said it was a very painful process. He said he was trying to set down things as they should have been. How we all must bear the responsibility for what had happened."

Mark's suspicions about Eckstein collided with this tale of the encounters in the gasthaus, the fragments whirling around his mind; Bühler, Zeimer, Eckstein, perhaps all heteronyms of one person. "What do you think he meant by 'should have been'?"

"You cannot know the world and the times he lived in. And he was a poet. So it was natural that after the War – when he had been engaged in some official bureaucratic work, which was completely counter to his artistic nature – he would want to write in a way that expressed his true self."

"We seem to be talking about two different truths. An historical truth and a fictional truth of regret – no, of remorse – a fantasy which would somehow exonerate you for your complicity in terrible crimes."

"You still do not understand, do you Mr Shilton. How so many were sucked down into a ... a vortex of involvement, in the stranglehold which those criminals and thugs laid on our poor Austria. And you cannot understand how, when it was all over, when the regime had been swept away, it was like coming out of a deep dark tunnel into the light, into the fresh air. At last we could all breath again and Bühler could begin to write again as he wished and to show what should have happened."

"Should have happened?"

"Yes, should! Bühler shouldered his share of all our guilt. He was perhaps no better than the average man on the Ringstrasse tram. He had a vision of what he might have been, of what he wished could have been if he had not been swept along by the torrent of events."

Mark was now thrown into a morass of doubt but decided to continue to address Eckstein as Bühler. "But you could have resisted, could have swum against that torrent."

"I tell you yet again. You do not – cannot – will never understand."

"And what about your family – the family you left in such desperate circumstances?"

"I have no family."

They both sat in silence for some while. A tannoy broadcast an announcement and a few moments later a small commuter train slid alongside the furthest platform. No-one got out or boarded the carriages and the train pulled out of the station towards the terminus. Mark looked intently at Eckstein and made a last attempt to unveil his true identity.

"Admit it, then, that you are Otto Bühler."

Eckstein sat with his head in his hands staring at the ground. "It is true that I knew Bühler, perhaps better than his brother Karl. I like to believe that I understood him through those talks in the gaststube and through his poetry and stories." And then in a hoarse whisper which Mark had to strain to catch, "Can't you understand. Zeimer is the real Bühler – you have ruined the remembrance of a life – you have twisted and distorted the testament of a poet. Go now – please go – I never want to see you again. You have taken his life and destroyed it!"

Mark dimly saw that Eckstein was suffering a self-imposed penance, in exile and poverty, for Bühler's actions while Zeimer lived on as his literary alter ego carrying his lost hopes for a purer past. Mark understood at last the pain he had inflicted. He felt a sudden urge to reach out to Eckstein and touch his shoulder, at least in a gesture of understanding, acknowledging the deep emotions which he had stirred up. But he stayed his hand before it touched the old man. Quietly he got to his feet and left, pausing only for a moment at the top of the stairs to look back at the figure, now strangely sunken, still staring at the ground.

Ten

"Do you really believe that he is Bühler?" asked Ruth after Mark had told her of his encounter at the station.

"I really don't know – yes, I'm confused about it. He certainly maintains the Eckstein role, always referring to Bühler in the third person. He certainly seems to have a detailed knowledge of Bühler's life. But somehow the descriptions of the meetings in the gasthaus had a rather novelistic ring. And then there are all those minor, circumstantial crumbs of evidence which seem to support my theory. " He shrugged. "It's thin stuff."

Ruth sat thoughtfully for a while. "If he is Bühler, why on earth would he come forward and break cover, so to speak. It would be stupid thing to do, and potentially dangerous."

"I know – I've been wondering about that. Maybe he now feels safe after over forty years in his new persona here in London. I think he needed to meet me to try and find out why I had changed the plot of his novel. He feels deeply wounded and needed to confront his accuser."

"He certainly seems worried enough about your identification of him with these threats about unmasking you."

"Yes but if he's not Bühler it may just be that there were some irregularities about his original arrival in Britain or maybe there are other reasons for not wanting the authorities to investigate him. You know – tax or something."

"So are you convinced?"

"He seems to have these two personas. Perhaps he is both Bühler and Eckstein. He has completely assumed his new identity and the self of forty years ago has become disconnected – has become somehow separated."

"So if you are convinced, are you going to report him to the authorities?"

"Report him? What do you mean?"

"Report him to the police or to the Wiesenthal organisation."

"Why – I don't quite understand. As an illegal immigrant or something?"

"No Mark, don't you see. He is a war criminal!"

"War criminal! He may be guilty of writing a novel which in effect whitewashed his past, but 'war criminal'! He was just one of the hundreds, of the thousands, who were drawn into supporting the regime during the War."

"But Mark, that's just the Nuremburg defence – 'he was only obeying orders'. It won't wash and never has done."

"But he had a pathetically minor role in what went on. He did no more than the signal men, the telegraph operators, the dispatch riders. OK, they were all complicit in a general sort of way but couldn't be classed as war criminals."

"If those who had played a so-called 'minor role' had stood up, had resisted in some way, or at least opted out of complicity, maybe the system would have collapsed. They all bear a level of responsibility. Evil might be 'banal' but it's still evil."

"OK, maybe Eckstein or Bühler does bear some responsibility but he is no candidate for a war crimes trial. He wasn't a sadistic camp guard or doctor conducting obscene experiments on prisoners."

"Who are you to decide that? You can't just set yourself up as judge and jury – or the prosecution service. It is up to them to decide, not you."

"I really can't agree. He was just a bit player in that tragedy like so many other thousands of minor officials."

"So you aren't going to take any action about your discovery – or at least your suspicions?"

"I don't know, Ruth. I need to think about it."

They let the matter drop and nothing was said in the next few days but Mark felt a change of atmosphere between them. A gap had opened up and the climate had become cooler. He turned Ruth's arguments over in his mind, developing counter-arguments and new factors to influence the debate. And why was she so convinced that Eckstein was Bühler?

If Eckstein really was Bühler he had already paid a price by leaving his family for the life of an impoverished immigrant in London. Mark felt that he had already delivered a harsh enough judgement and carried out the punishment of rewriting the defendant's novel. He had genuinely appeared deeply affected by the recasting of the plot. Enough to make Mark himself question what he had done and from what position of moral authority he had proceeded. Meanwhile his deep anxiety about being unmasked over the change in the novel's plot resurfaced. Eckstein's threat had emphasised his precarious position poised above the abyss of professional nemesis. Each morning now he woke with a vague but persistent sense of dread.

One afternoon while travelling back home from a meeting, Mark was waiting on the Underground platform at Baker Street when a loud speaker crackled into life. "The Piccadilly line is part suspended between Kings Cross and Arnos Grove due to a person under a train at Finsbury Park."

As he stared absent minded at an advertisement on the far side of the track, the announcement gradually filtered into his consciousness. His vague sense of responsibility for what seemed Eckstein's despair suddenly focussed. 'A person under a train' – 'you have taken a life'. Eckstein had committed suicide or attempted to. After a moment's frozen realization, Mark's imperative to action released him. He tried to work out an alternative Underground route to Finsbury Park but gave up. Speed was essential. He ran up the escalator and out onto Marylebone Road. The third taxi which he hailed pulled over and set off with Mark in an agony of apprehension. The taxi crawled through the clotted traffic which only eased on reaching the Euston underpass. He was aware of time rushing by, the minute hand of his watch moving relentlessly forward, as he pleaded with the driver, explaining the urgency of the journey. Just before St Pancras, the driver turned left and they were in a maze of cobbled lanes between grim engine houses. As the taxi ran along the bank of the Grand Union Canal, the phrase 'taken his own life' came back to him. Bühler had taken his life and created a new one in Eckstein. Now Eckstein had finally taken his own life and Mark had been the trigger for that final act. Suddenly after passing under a low railway bridge, the taxi turned right threading its way through a maze of back streets then a grid of quiet residential roads as the driver worked his way north east towards Finsbury Park.

Finally arriving at the station, the taxi pulled in behind an ambulance. Mark thrust some notes at the driver, leapt out and sprinted to the station entrance. A policewoman stood in front of the closed metal grilles. Two ambulances were backed up to the entrance and he saw a group of paramedics bending over a stretcher by the back of one. A small crowd of onlookers were gathered at the edge of the scene. Pushing through the crowd and avoiding the policewoman, he rushed towards the ambulance but found his way blocked by a burly paramedic.

"I need to see him – I know him – a friend ..." spluttered Mark.

"I'm sorry sir, you can't – and it's not a 'him'. It's a young woman, early twenties, sir – now please stand back."

Mark felt a hand on his elbow and allowed himself to be led away by the policewoman as he retraced his steps trying to avoid the stares of the onlookers. Gradually, the adrenalin began to drain out of his blood and his breathing eased. Despite his embarrassed confusion, he felt a renewed sense of empathy for Eckstein. In all his research, his rewriting and his confrontation with him, he had experienced a growing closeness and a sense of responsibility for his fate. That fate still rested, undecided, in his hands.

He wandered away from the station, uncertain as to what to do next. In order to reassure himself finally that Eckstein was alive and well, he decided to visit him in his flat despite his plea to be left alone. Fonthill Road was deserted and litter blew along the pavement into the gutter. Mark carefully descended to the basement and pressed the cheap doorbell. There was no reply so he knocked loudly on the door. There were sounds from inside of the door being unlocked and it was slowly opened a little. Eckstein peered out. "I thought I made it clear, Mr Shilton, that I wished never to see you again."

"I ... I know. But I just wanted to make sure that ... that you were alright."

"I appreciate your concern, Mr Shilton. I am still here but I do not care for your interest." Mark was at a loss as to what to say next but suddenly remembered the final piece of information that Ella Taub had given him.

"I should have said before – I heard that Liesl Schiff survived."

The door opened a little wider so that Mark could see Eckstein more clearly. "Liesl Schiff – what about her?"

"She survived, went to America and married there. She lives in New Jersey."

He shrugged and pursed his lips. Mark strained to hear a whisper. "Liesl Schiff. In America?" He stared at Mark or through Mark as if down a long avenue, through a distant gateway, into a deep landscape of the past. He stood motionless, peering out of his doorway for some moments silhouetted with the light behind him. Mark could not be certain but did he glimpse a wet cheek? Slowly the door closed and the latch clicked shut.

Mark mounted the few steps to the pavement and made his way through a grid of streets without any clear plan or direction. He still had no clear evidence that Eckstein was Bühler but his intuition was as strong as his doubts. He now felt a deep understanding of how events had shaped that life, and mundane human weakness had led to his failures and crimes. Had he imagined Eckstein's tear and did it reveal real remorse or only maudlin regret? Was he capable of redemption? As Mark walked slowly up the street, the sun warming his back, he mused about the afternoon's events. Could an individual be two; two conflicting ways of being which would indicate not hypocrisy but a fundamental need for integration and an attempt to exorcise whatever lay in the shadows of the past.

Pausing to cross a busy junction, he noticed that he was close to Landseer Road. It was there that he and Elizabeth had shared an upstairs flat and where, during a long hot summer, Katy was conceived. The memory of that time, when they were young and creating their own world together was now so painful that he took an involuntary gasp of breath and stood motionless on the kerb for some time. Were they happy then? He found it difficult to remember exactly. Perhaps happiness cannot be recalled but only experienced in the moment.

"So your little Nazi friend hadn't topped himself." Ruth's voice had a grating edge to it. "I'm not sure whether that would have been natural justice or an escape from justice."

Mark remained silent under her gaze, uncertain how to respond to her vehemence.

"And have you made up your mind about reporting him?"

Mark did not reply immediately to her interrogation. He suddenly felt very tired. "No, I haven't decided yet. I must admit that I find it very difficult. You know my views about his culpability – a very small cog in that dreadful machine. But more than that, I believe he is genuinely remorseful about his involvement. His novel is a statement, a cry even, of what he hoped to have been. And I believe he has suffered, perhaps sufficiently, for what he did. His paranoia about the revenge groups led him to leave his family and hide in the country living in obscurity and poverty. He managed to get to London where he has led a lonely, rather pathetic life. I think he has paid in measure – maybe not in full measure but measure enough."

Ruth gazed at him with her chin on her hand. "I cannot understand why you have become some sort of advocate for this awful little creep. Why are you so ready to apologise for him? I think you feel guilty for changing the plot of his novel and believe that your crazy idea has solved everything, that he has been punished, so everything is over and done with."

Mark felt the blows of her charges and tried to think clearly and honestly. "There is another aspect of his guilt." He avoided Ruth's eyes and tried to marshal his thoughts. "Eckstein always refers to Bühler in the third person. Now that might be just a technique to avoid being unmasked. But I believe that there is a clear psychological break between the two. Bühler escaped from Vienna, wrote a novel of self-justification and then died. So Bühler vanishes and Eckstein is created. He moves to England and builds a new life – a life which is his own." He paused and saw that she was listening intently. "How far can guilt pursue us? If I stole something when I was eighteen, am I still guilty of that 'crime' thirty five years later? I am a totally different person from that young man who, OK, bore my name. There is no connection between old man Eckstein and the misguided young poet Bühler."

"What crap!" She spat out the words. "I don't understand how your sense of moral responsibility could be so distorted. These are trendy ideas about the transitory experience of individuality and the nature of the self. Firstly, you dare to compare some theoretical minor theft with complicity in the murder of tens of thousands. Then you suggest that we are not responsible for our actions just because some time has passed."

He realized that this argument could not be easily resolved. "I don't know why you are getting so upset about this." He looked up. Her eyes had widened in a state of shock. The moment balanced on the blade of a knife.

She spoke softly and slowly but with a tightly controlled intensity which distorted her voice. "I will tell you why I am upset. My parents came to London from Poland in 1938. They are Jews, my father from Krakow, my mother from Katowice. They met here and fell in love. My father joined the RAF and flew in the Polish squadron. After the war, they got married and I was born a couple of years later. Now, Mark, listen. I have no aunts or uncles, no cousins. I never knew my grandparents – that thread is broken. All, yes all, were swept away. All were herded into wagons organised, with great efficiency, by some ordinary official, just like your Otto Bühler. You know, Primo Levi said somewhere that there is a train in every story. Now do you understand why I get upset when you defend your little Nazi friend."

Mark remained silent, nodding mechanically. They had never shared their family histories but now the significance of her Friday suppers with her parents was clear. It explained so much of her attitude and arguments. Now she had paused for a moment, her breath coming in short gasps as she paced up and down the room, her hands clenched together. "One year we went back to Poland, my parents and I. We went to where they had lived but they found no-one they remembered – or who remembered them. They were both terribly upset, my father very much so. He had always felt so guilty that he had not arranged for his parents to get away in time. That guilt still colours his life. And maybe I've inherited some of that too."

Mark began to realise that her history shed a new piercing light on his views of Bühler's responsibility. But Ruth had not finished. "Look into your own heart, Mark. You are dogged by some problem in the past. I don't know what it is. But it haunts you – that much I do know. I think your remorse or guilt has somehow become an excuse for Bühler's. You don't feel able to judge him because you too are morally compromised!"

Mark leapt to his feet, gave her a wild look, and ran down the stairs, slamming the front door. He had to get out, get away from all these truths, all the burden of the past breaking out and shattering any certainties. He strode down the street kicking through the first autumn leaves and litter. He had to get air, get space, and escape Ruth's inquisition.

He found himself in a small public garden, a patch of scuffed grass in the shadow of a looming Victorian church. He stumbled across the grass avoiding the litter and dog faeces to a bench beneath the tall grimy wall of the church pierced by a rose window covered in rusty metal netting. He ignored a group of street drinkers on far side of the garden and sat for a while staring unseeing at the ground, his hands tightly clenched together. How had Ruth sensed his loss and unearthed his guilt over leaving Elizabeth? In the encroaching dusk, the flood gates of memory opened. Her haggard, pleading face and little Katy, crying as her world disintegrated, clinging not to him but to her mother. His grief over Jamie's death closing him off, unable to support Elizabeth, until he had to get away. Confronting his isolation and loneliness, he realized it was in Ruth that he sought redemption and comfort. Now, finally, he came to acknowledge his own failure and guilt, his inability to transcend his deep grief and provide the love and support which might have healed the family of their terrible loss. Suddenly he was racked by deep, uncontrollable sobs which shook his whole body as he sat hunched on the bench, overwhelmed by waves of emotion.

Suddenly he felt a hand on his shoulder. "You a'right luv?" He looked up to see a thin woman with long hair streaked with green and tattoos from wrist to shoulder. "You OK?" she thrust a can of cider towards him. He stared up at her uncomprehending and shook his head. Stumbling away, he recalled Ella Taub's account of Bühler's desertion of his family. So Ruth had been more perceptive than she realized when she suggested that he felt linked to Bühler through their shared cowardice. And now he needed to come to terms with Ruth's Jewish inheritance and the way it had altered the whole context of his dilemma over Eckstein. All he could feel was an urgent need to be with Ruth; to re-establish their ability to talk calmly about the mundane business of life and for her to tell him that she cared for him and forgave him his confusion.

It was quite dark now and a thin rain had started to fall as he slowly retraced his steps towards the flat. He paused at the doorway of the local pub, wondering whether a drink would steady his nerves, and entered the noisy, smoke-filled room. He was jostled as he tried to get to the bar and eventually found himself staring at the barmaid who was waiting for his order. Suddenly he felt an overwhelming urge to get away from the crowding drinkers and their shouted conversations. With a shrug, he turned away and pushed through the press of bodies towards the door.

As he wearily climbed the stairs to the flat he found Ruth waiting for him. "Where have you been all this time? I was worried about you." She gently stroked his cheek.

"I didn't know about your family – I'm so sorry."

"How could you know – we've shared so little of our pasts."

"Well, now I need to think this whole business through. After all the re-writing and then meeting Eckstein, I've ... well perhaps, become confused. I can't seem to see the whole picture properly. And I'm sorry – deeply sorry to have upset you."

Mark sat on the sofa, the pain of this new distance from Ruth rising in his chest. She pulled over a chair and sat before him, staring intently. He met her eyes trying to discern whether they held contempt or compassion.

"Mark, your support for Eckstein or Bühler is a major problem for me. I cannot understand it and it somehow strikes deep into me. It's not just that I'm upset. It seems that there may be some fundamental incompatibility between us. If we see the world, see the past, in such utterly different ways, then at a deep level we may not be able to communicate. It's no good if we can chat about the latest film or local restaurant but not be in some sort of accord about our basic beliefs and agree about what's right and what's wrong."

Mark sat silently, listening to her homily. A welter of ideas and emotions surged through his head. "It's not that I really support Eckstein. It's just that after all the research and writing – and meeting him, I sort of see things through his eyes."

"Have you thought that he could be highly manipulative? It would certainly fit in with his history. Whatever the reasons, I'm afraid that this has really changed the way I see you. I don't know yet whether I can be with this new understanding of you, now that all has been peeled back."

The breath drained out of him, the pressure of his emotions suffocating him. All the certainties of his existence whirled about him as if the flat itself, its walls and slates, had disintegrated and were blown like autumn leaves in a vicious gust of wind.

For two days, he moved in a trance, numbed at the realization that their relationship had suffered perhaps irreparable damage. He knew that these issues had to be resolved and a decision taken but could not find the energy or courage to tackle them. After yet another silent breakfast, he could not stay and work in the flat even after Ruth had left for her school. He found an empty desk at the library and started on some translation work which he had put off for a week. He could not concentrate but sat back in his chair gazing up at the galleried shelving and shafts of sunlight piercing the gloom. The familiar ache of anxiety about Ruth and their life together knotted his stomach. His overriding need was to ensure that they could be together for the future so that a life with her would allow him to live again, to live fully, and to redeem the past.

Slowly he picked through the evidence of the previous year; his discovery of Bühler's wartime activities and his flight from both his family and the scene of his crimes. He pondered on the effect of the recasting of the Zeimer persona had had on Eckstein and to what extent his exile had been a penance for what he had perpetrated. Mark wondered whether, as Ruth had suggested, Eckstein had manipulated him. The pact over mutual silence had somehow underlain his whole relationship with him, at times almost forgotten but always colouring any views on future action. And now, amongst all this moral confusion, two simple issues became quite clear in his mind. He had to be prepared to sacrifice his carefully nurtured career in order to retain, or indeed regain, Ruth's love and affection in a future which beckoned so urgently. For that love, all must be sacrificed, his respected position among colleagues and clients, and Eckstein himself, redeemed or unredeemed. All must be cast aside in his overriding need for the security and hope which he believed Ruth could, and would provide.

Eleven

The interview room at Paddington Green Police Station was minimalist to a fault. Grey, scuffed walls devoid of posters or any decoration enclosed a square of dirty lino. Mark shifted on his hard metal framed chair and looked across the formica tabletop at Detective Constable Thompson who was writing in a large report book.

"And what is the basis of your suspicion that this Mr Eckstein might be a certain Mr Bühler?" Despite the smallness of the room, its hard surfaces created a strange acoustic deadening effect so that Mark had to lean forward and strain to hear the detective's words.

"Well – in my conversations with him."

"I take it that he has not admitted changing his name."

"No he hasn't – but he seems to know a lot about Mr Bühler's life and family."

Mark detailed all the links which he had picked up in his conversations with Eckstein, explaining how they tied back to known facts about Bühler's life. As he did so, he became aware of the thin basis of his assertions and as he itemised the clues, he realised how farfetched it must seem. He had decided that his dream and the plum pastry connection might not provide convincing evidence. All the while, DC Thompson carefully wrote down Mark's explanations.

"I see – but you are convinced that Mr Eckstein is in fact Mr Bühler?"

"Yes – yes, I am."

"And you claim that Mr Bühler was – or is – a war criminal."

"Yes – that's right."

"And this claim is based on ...?"

"Mainly as a result of interviewing an old friend of Mr Bühler's – a Herr Herlinger."

This detail was laboriously copied down into the report book. "And Mr Her ... Herlinger provided testimony that Mr Bühler was involved in the transportation of Jews from Vienna in 1942?" Mark nodded.

"Can you provide Mr Herlinger's contact details, please?"

"Yes. He lives in Trieste."

"Tree-est? That in Italy? I see, hmm, – that'll be a problem."

Finally he looked up and asked, "Is there anything else that you think might be relevant to the case, Sir?"

He could think of nothing more that might support his allegation and could not avoid being aware of the detective's air of weary scepticism about his account. The whole process had had begun to undermine his own certainty of the Bühler-Eckstein link. Was it only a product of a fevered imagination brought on by his obsession with Bühler?

"Well, in that case, Sir, we will initiate some enquiries. If we need to ask you to come in again for any further information, we will get in touch with you."

He was not sure if the interview was over as the detective continued to scan his report book. He then became aware that he was being closely scrutinised.

"How did you meet Mr Eckstein, Sir?"

"He got in touch with me about a translation I had carried out."

"He contacted you?"

"Yes that's right."

"About a translation?"

"Yes – I had translated a novel by Mr Bühler." Mark felt a frisson of danger. He could not bring himself to reveal the changes to the plot.

"And did Mr Eckstein criticize your translation?"

"Well ... I suppose ...yes, in a way."

"In what sort of a way?"

"Well, he just didn't agree with some parts of the translation."

"And did that upset you?"

"No ... but, I suppose no-one likes criticism, do they."

The detective did not reply and in the long silence which followed, Mark became aware of the sound of distant traffic and then shouting at the far end of the corridor outside the room and of a heavy door being slammed.

"Mr Shilton, I am sure you are aware that making a false allegation against a person is a very serious offence."

As Mark emerged from the police station into the roar of traffic on the Edgware Road, he found that his shirt was soaked with sweat. If the police could not find sufficient evidence for the Eckstein-Bühler link, he might face prosecution. Meanwhile Eckstein would have revealed all to Thalia and his career would be utterly ruined. His fate was now in the hands of others. A sense of complete resignation overwhelmed him. Only his desperate hope for a future with Ruth provided the faintest glimmer of optimism.

Ruth listened carefully to his account of the interview and hugged him with tears in her eyes. She appeared gratified that he had finally taken the action which she had pressed upon him but Mark wondered if her response hid an underlying grudging concern that he had been pushed into taking action. He just hoped that now their relationship could recover and return to the warmer atmosphere they had enjoyed in past months, especially during their stay in Wales.

But how close had they been then? What he had taken for companionable silences were times when she withdrew, wrapped in self-absorption and beyond any communication. Some evenings, he now remembered, she had gone to bed early leaving him reading by the embers of the fire. In the morning, he would wake to find her gone and once, in a moment of panic, went to the window to see her returning along the cliff path. She was pulling her waterproof tightly around her against the fine rain, not glancing out at the grey waves but with unseeing eyes fixed on the path ahead.

A week later a different detective rang from Paddington Green police station. "Mr Shilton? I wonder if you could assist us in the case of a Mr Eckstein who you reported to a colleague of mine? Officers have visited the address on two occasions but have not managed to speak to him. Do you know if he is on holiday or away for some reason?" Mark confessed that he knew nothing of Eckstein's whereabouts but would see what he could do to assist the investigation.

He felt vaguely resentful at being drawn back into the police enquiry. He had hoped to distance himself and calmly await the verdict on Eckstein's, and his own, future. After mulling over the problem for a while, he decided that the only useful action would be to visit, yet again, the flat on Fonthill Road.

Next day he arrived at the tall villa, its stucco crumbling even more noticeably, and negotiated the steps, slippery with moss, to the basement flat. To his surprise, the front door was slightly ajar. He tentatively pushed it open and stepped inside. The entrance gave into a narrow hall and a doorway led off right into the main living room. The room was barely furnished and otherwise empty except for a man standing and jotting down details onto a clipboard. He turned to stare truculently at Mark. "Hello – can I help you?"

"I was looking for Mr Eckstein."

"Gone. Left sometime last week."

"Can you tell me where ... where I can get in touch with him?"

"Haven't a clue – just disappeared. Paid a month's rent, cleaned the place up a bit and was gone. No forwarding address."

"I see." Mark stood uncertain of what to do or say.

"You a friend of his or chasing an unpaid bill?"

"No, no – just a friend. I had hoped to have a word with him."

"Well, if you want you can have a look through this. If he's your friend, you can take what you like. The lot's going into the bin." He gestured with his foot to a cardboard box and shoved it across the floor in Mark's direction. He peered into it. It contained the pathetic remains of Eckstein's simple life in the flat. A well used saucepan, a cracked mug, some tarnished cutlery and a tin box were discernable. He picked up the tin box and prised it open but it only contained a few tea bags. As he was about to replace it, he noticed a copy of 'Hidden in the Shadows' lying at the bottom of the box. He picked it up and quickly flipped through the pages, aware that the man was watching. He noticed that those sections of the book which included major changes from the original had been annotated with a broad brown crayon mark down the edge of the page.

"May I take this?" He held out the book.

"No problem, 'course you can." After a pause during which he stared at Mark quizzically, "You an old friend of Mr E?"

"Sort of – I feel I've known him for a long time."

"Funny that he didn't let you know he was going."

"Yes, it is a bit odd." And after a moment's thought, "He was always a very private person."

"You can say that again. Now, if you'll excuse me, I've got to get on checking the furniture and contents."

Mark thanked him and left the flat, pausing at the top of the steps to look down at the book which he clutched tightly in his hand.

Back at home, Mark tried to disentangle his thoughts about Eckstein's disappearance. His first inclination was to worry that now he was in hiding, Eckstein could make the recasting of the book's plot public. On reflection, this seemed unlikely as any approach to the publisher or others would jeopardise his own security. He wondered why he had chosen this moment to make a run for it. Perhaps he had become increasingly concerned about Mark's ability to reveal his true identity. He may have become aware of the visits by the police to his flat and decided that the time had come to leave.

Mark managed to get through to DC Thompson. "Well, thank you for letting us know, Sir. We'll get Immigration to put a stop order at exit ports. And we'll keep the file very much open. We'll get in touch with you if there are developments." Mark thanked him but felt that he heard in the detective's voice a note of relief that this problematic case could be shelved and, did he imagine it, a tinge of contempt.

"Eckstein's gone – left his flat." Ruth looked up, her wide eyes questioning him for more information.

"Any clues as to where he's gone?"

"None. He paid the rent and literally cleared out."

"Why d'you think he decided to disappear now?"

"Don't know – but there are all sorts of possible reasons."

"I wonder where he's gone to. Could he have picked up some remark of yours – about reporting him."

"No, of course not." He was hurt that she could imagine him as somehow complicit in Eckstein's flight.

"All those visits to his flat. You might easily have tipped him off without being explicit. This sort of empathy you seem to have with him."

"No ... no! Our pact of silence reassured him rather than scared him off." He realised that his sacrifices to retain her regard for him were still deeply undermined by a lack of trust. He turned moodily away and went into the kitchen to pour himself a drink.

In the weeks that followed, their relationship continued with a new flavour, perhaps less close, certainly more realistic. Each had learnt more and understood the flaws and weaknesses of the other. They now knew a little of each other's past and the way it seeped into the present. He found her rigid certainties difficult to understand and the unpredictable changes in mood made him draw back in fear of alienating her by his advances. He could only guess at her feelings for him. At times she was still affectionate, reaching out physically and emotionally for him. She could also be withdrawn, apparently ignoring him or even seeming unaware of his existence.

At breakfast one day, Ruth suddenly said, "I've found a new flat – it seems just what I've been looking for."

Mark looked up, his cup poised between table and lips. "Why ...?" His voice trailed away leaving the unarticulated question lying between them.

She frowned and got up from the table and went to stand looking out of the window at the early morning rush in the street below. After some moments, she spoke in a quiet, somehow distant voice, "When we got together, it sort of happened that we didn't talk about the past. I can't remember if that was explicit or just something that happened. At the time it seemed right. But looking back now – I don't know. There never seemed a right moment to drag these things out. But I think we were wrong. So much baggage – so much unsaid – sort of lurking there."

"But what is it that ...?"

"No, no – I'm not going into it all now, not now. It's too late – far too late."

"But just some sort of explanation!"

"Yes, I do realise. You deserve some ... reason." She stood staring out of the window now flecked with rain. Eventually, "I've been through a very bad time – a very dark place. Something happened and I once gave up everything, even part of myself – and I can't forgive myself for that. And now I have to keep on the move – any sort of permanence terrifies me – a sort of claustrophobia. I'm sorry – I daren't say more than that. And I know I owe you more – I'm sorry – so sorry."

She was still turned away from him and he could barely see her profile silhouetted against the light.

"And Bühler?" he asked, "has Bühler got something to do with this?"

She was silent for a while. "Yes – I suppose he is a factor. My moral world is very black and white. I see everything as a conflict between good and evil. Very simplistic, very naïve, you may say. But that's how I see things. Maybe my parents handed it down to me – I don't know. But you, Mark, see the moral world in shades of grey. That's not meant as a criticism. It's just the way you see it. Maybe it's more realistic – the way the world really is. Although it makes decisions more difficult."

"So you're leaving."

"Yes. I still have to sign the lease and tidy up a few details. But in about ten days." He drew in his lips and bit down on them. Silently, he began to clear away breakfast and left her still staring out of the window. He was drained of all emotions save for an emptiness and a sense of utter aloneness, his life now bare and stretching to a horizon bereft of hope.

It was agreed that Ruth would move out while Mark was away in Birmingham for a couple of days attending a conference. In their few remaining days together they found reasons to leave the flat early or return late. Meals were mainly eaten in silence. After all he had sacrificed: his risk of exposure and prosecution, Bühler himself, and even his moral intuitions, confused as they were, all for her love, he felt betrayed and cheated. They still shared the same bed but when he reached out to touch her tentatively she would only hold his hand and squeeze it; no more.

When Mark returned from Birmingham, he climbed the stairs slowly, dreading to enter the flat which would proclaim her absence. Everything was neat and tidy; she appeared to have cleaned the rooms after removing all her belongings and had even replaced a pile of books and a German beer mug in positions she must have remembered when she first visited the flat. On the table in the living room was an expensive looking bottle of claret against which was propped a note on a piece of paper torn from an exercise book. In her girlish handwriting, he read:

'Dear Mark, thank you so much for everything – I'll never forget the last few months. Ruth'

Underneath, as an afterthought, in a barely legible scrawl, he managed to decipher: *'You have been so very kind my dear and I have been very hard on you – forgive.'*

He tore the note up slowly into ever smaller pieces until they fell, fading petals, onto the table. He felt no anger but a bitter sweet regret. He went into the kitchen to fetch a corkscrew and wineglass. He crumpled into the sofa and drank the first glass of the good wine, thinking over all that had happened since he first met Ruth and then discovered Bühler. He thought about how Bühler had been drawn into the grinding machinery that had engulfed and processed so many lives and finally annihilated them. He imagined Bühler working with his timetables and telephones deep in the department in Vienna. And then, Ruth's wide family and community packed into crude wagons travelling East and always returning empty. The waves of those terrible events had spread far and wide until the insidious ripples had even touched his own life and helped break apart his relationship with Ruth, destroying his hopes of happiness. Both Ruth and Ella Taub, daughters of victims and perpetrator, had inherited a portion of guilt and pain, passed on down the generations. As he finished the last glass of the now empty bottle, he could no longer hold back the tears of self-pity, swiftly followed by tears of self-contempt.

He slept late then wandered around the flat, the rooms strangely enlarged and echoing. Distracted, he began to tidy some shelves, moving stacks of papers and thrusting them into a cupboard. Seizing a pile of books, he began pushing them, randomly into any space in the bookcase. He found himself holding Eckstein's copy of 'Hidden in the Shadows' and idly flipped through it. At the end of the book, between two blank pages, was something he had not noticed before. He gingerly extracted it to find a black and white photograph slightly creased and dog-eared. It showed two figures, a young man and woman laughing in front of some imposing building. Something seemed vaguely familiar about it and then he suddenly remembered the carnival photograph which Frau Bühler had shown him. This must have been taken on the same occasion. There was the young Bühler, recognisable from the picture he had found in the Austrian Cultural Institute. He turned it over. On the back in a copybook gothic script he read, '*Otto, Vergissmeinicht, Lisa.*'

Epilogue

'Upon this bank and shoal of time'
Shakespeare – *Macbeth*

A cold wind is sweeping rain before it along the Strand and whirling around the Aldwich. The annual Johansen Lecture at King's has just drawn to a close, the applause dying away, and Mark is shuffling out of the hall with the crowd. He finds himself jostled within a few feet of Jeremy Garforth and returning his grin.

"I hear the Bühler book is doing well.'"

"Yes, rather gratifying."

"After all your editorial work!"

"Jeremy – what are you talking about?" He cannot quite decide whether a flicker of Jeremy's right eye is a wink or nervous tic.

They are swirled apart by the press of people pushing forward into the lobby. Mark wanders among the talking groups gathered around the tables of drinks and canapés. He is transfixed when a gap reveals across the room a woman in a striking yellow dress with shoulder length blond hair, her face half turned away. Something in the shape of her cheek and the movement of her head holds his attention. It is Elizabeth; not as she must be now but as she was thirty or so years ago when he loved her so tenderly, so desperately. He almost makes an involuntary move towards her but she turns and is a stranger.

Mark leans over a table spread with food among glasses of wine and begins to load a plate. "I hope that's not going to be your supper, Mark!" He turns to face a smiling Ruth and stifles a quick in-drawing of breath. He smiles, searching for words. "How's everything?" Mundane news is exchanged as if they are mere acquaintances with no history. A younger woman with dark bobbed hair, wearing a designer jacket and jeans comes up to stand by Ruth. As their shoulders touch, she turns her head slightly and Mark notices her eyes widen and the suggestion of a smile play on her lips. In that instant a strange blend of affection and regret allows him to understand the extent of his loss.

"Angela, this is Mark." He shakes the proffered hand. "Any news of your little ... er ... Austrian friend?"

"No – not a word. Quite disappeared off the face of the earth."

"What a funny business."

"Yes – quite a business."

Mark stares down at his glass of wine as a curious mixture of pain and happiness surge through him. The past and future, Ruth and Bühler, Elizabeth and himself, all threads woven and knotted together as a continuous corded rope stretched in time and yet timeless hover at the edge of his consciousness. He smiles again, hoping they will not see the tears which give the whole room a distant, unreal quality, "It was great to see you again, bye!"

Over lunch they discuss Katy's plans to travel to eastern Europe during her summer holidays. Now that the Wall is down, she wants to see what is happening in Berlin and Prague for herself and meet the young people there. This is the second time that she has come to join him for lunch on a Sunday and Mark hopes that perhaps a monthly ritual might be growing. It gives him an opportunity to get to know this young woman he had only remembered as a little girl. His deepest hope is that her return is a gesture of forgiveness for his desertion and perhaps an understanding of what happened between her parents, even if all that is lost is irrecoverable.

With lunch barely finished, she jumps to her feet and announces that she has to be off. "And while I'm away, you'll look after Mum?"

"Yes."

"You really will?"

"Yes – yes, of course."

Grabbing her coat and rucksack, she gives him a quick peck on the cheek and rushes headlong down the stairs. The front door bangs shut and at the window he watches his daughter half run down the street, tugging the rucksack straps over her shoulders.

The deep quiet of a Sunday afternoon envelopes the street. The flat is hushed, exhaling its emptiness. He stays at the window, leaning his forehead against the cool glass, unseeing and unthinking. Very faintly, through tiny vibrations in the glass, he feels more than hears a distant train hammer rhythmically over the rails and then a louder clatter as it crosses some points. For a moment the strange anxiety of his journey back from Trieste surfaces. He wonders where Bühler is now. Perhaps in Argentina or even back in Austria. Maybe he has only moved south of the river and is sitting at this moment on a platform at Clapham Junction, checking the trains against the timetable. And then, Liesl Schiff in a retirement home in New Jersey. When her grandchildren come to visit, does she wear long sleeves or perhaps a broad bangle to hide the indelible numbers on her wrist? From far away, the dying fall of a train klaxon and in his mind's eye a long line of closed wagons moves slowly out of the Nordbahnhof marshalling yards, departing Vienna.

The Author

J.M. Taylor held posts in Berlin and Vienna
during the Cold War. He is co-author of a detailed
account of a nineteenth century battle in SW France.
He now lives in London.